BEYOND

A GHOST STORY

graham mcnamee

WENDY
LAMB
BOOKS

The author acknowledges the support of the Canada Council for the Arts.

All rights reserved. Published in the United States by Wendy Lamb Books, an imprint of Random House Children's Books, a division of Random House, Inc., New York.

Wendy Lamb Books and the colophon are trademarks of Random House, Inc.

Visit us on the Web! randomhouse.com/teens

Educators and librarians, for a variety of teaching tools, visit us at RHTeachersLibrarians.com

Library of Congress Cataloging-in-Publication Data
McNamee, Graham.
Beyond : a ghost story / by Graham McNamee. — 1st ed.
p. cm.
Summary: Everyone thinks seventeen-year-old Jane has attempted suicide more than once, but Jane knows the truth: her shadow is trying to kill her.
ISBN 978-0-385-73775-3 (trade) — ISBN 978-0-385-90687-6 (lib. bdg.) —
ISBN 978-0-375-89759-7 (ebook) — ISBN 978-0-375-85165-0 (pbk.) [1. Near-death experiences—Fiction. 2. Ghosts—Fiction.] I. Title.
PZ7.M232519 Be 2012
[Fic]—dc23
2011043610

Printed in the United States of America

10 9 8 7 6 5 4 3 2 1

First Edition

BEYOND

A GHOST STORY

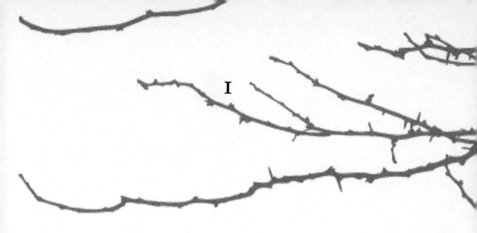

I

I remember dying.

After I got injured my heart stopped and I flatlined.

I was done and gone. But I wasn't alone.

There was something waiting for me when I died. Something dark and cold tried to take my soul away.

When they brought me back to life I escaped from it. Left it behind.

But what if it came back with me, followed me home like a hungry stray?

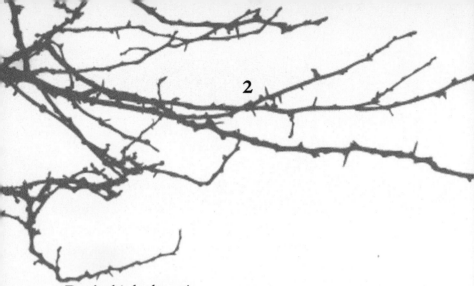

Don't think about it.

I keep telling myself that.

Today I find out what they're going to do with me. I'm counting down the hours till my doctor's appointment.

My best friend, Lexi, is doing her best to distract me. So on this stormy afternoon she drags me out in my backyard to try a new trick shot with her camera. "We're going to stop the rain."

That would be a real magic trick out here on the Rain Coast, in the town of Edgewood. Never heard of the place? I'm shocked. We're famous for our wet weather.

Lexi gets me to stand under the tree in back. It doesn't give me any shelter, with all the dripping branches.

"What do I do?" I ask as she sets up her tripod on the grass.

"Just stay still, Jane. Facing me. I need to get the focus perfect."

Most days are gray around here, where the sky is always crowded with clouds and the rainy season never seems to end. Makes you feel color-blind sometimes, starving your eyes. Only the bloodred of Lexi's lipstick saves the world from fading to black-and-white right now.

"Ready?" she says. "Okay, the camera's set for super-quick shots. Don't move for a minute. And close your eyes. This flash is really intense."

I shut them, and Lexi starts shooting as the wind shakes cold raindrops from the branches above. Through my lids I can make out the flashes, like rapid-fire lightning. When it feels like a minute's gone by, I open my eyes and catch the last blinding flares.

"Done," she says.

We run to the back porch and check out the results. As I blink away the afterimage fireworks, my vision clears and I see Lexi beside me.

Always in black, she looks like the Grim Reaper's hot little sister. Right now she's wearing a hooded slicker over her miniskirt and tight sweater. Raven-dark hair frames her pale face.

"Got it." She shows me the image on her camera. "Took a hundred shots to get it, but we tricked the rain."

There I am. Brown eyes wide, frizzy blond hair blown wild by the wind so it seems like I got zapped by lightning. Makes me look witchy.

But the magic is in how the raindrops are stopped in midair. They show up as streaks around me, but where the focus is tightest right in front of my face a few are frozen. Caught in the split-second flash, they seem solid, as if you could pluck one out of the air and hold it. Crystal clear pearls.

"You stopped the rain," I say.

Lexi shrugs it off. "A minor miracle."

"I could use a miracle right about now."

"The rain falls too fast to really *stop* it. But the drips from the branches are slowed down enough to catch." She hands me the camera. "Now you try."

We experiment some more, capturing the dribbles off the porch roof, suspended before gravity splashes them to the ground. Cool special effects.

But Lexi's best trick is to take my mind off everything. And it works wonders.

Playing with the camera lets me breathe for a while. Before everything unfreezes, the drops start falling again, and the clock counts down.

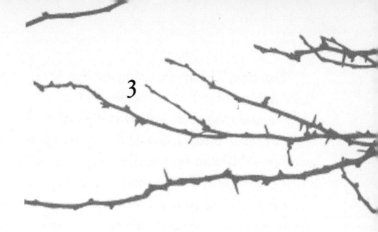

3

That's me.

The X-ray on the wall shows the ghost image of my skull. Me skeletonized. No eyes, no skin, no hair.

It's like seeing my reflection in Death's own mirror. Spooky.

The neurologist is talking to Mom and Dad, but I only catch fragments of what he's saying.

"No intracranial swelling . . . no bleeding . . . no infection . . . no change."

Skeletons are so anonymous. Hard to tell a guy from a girl, old from young. Stripped down to my bare bones, the only way I can really tell this is me is by that little white sliver buried inside the skull.

I'm so fascinated by my naked bones that it takes a few seconds before I realize Mom's talking to me.

"Jane?"

"Huh?"

"Do you have any questions?"

I glance at their faces, all grim and worried.

"Just one," I say, pointing to the X-ray. "Does this make me look fat?"

The neurologist frowns, Dad sighs, Mom looks pissed.

"What?" I shrug, like I can't help it. Nobody ever gets me. I mean, if I don't joke about this a little I'll curl up in a ball in my room and never come out.

"Okay, seriously then. Are you gonna cut the thing out, or will I be setting off metal detectors for the rest of my life?"

The doc glances down at my chart. "Eventually it will have to come out, but right now, the situation is stable. You're doing remarkably well. It might be more dangerous to go in and remove it. We'll have to run some additional tests."

Great. More tests.

They start going over all the pills I'm taking.

As the doc writes some new prescriptions, Mom grills him on side effects and complications.

I turn back to my X-ray. Lexi always said I was wrong in the head, and here's the proof. But really, I can't lay all my weirdness on that little white sliver there. I was twisted long before that showed up.

The nail in my brain.

On the drive home everybody's all silent and gloomy.

"Call off the funeral!" I say to break the tension. "I'm still breathing."

Mom grunts and shakes her head. Dad frowns at me in the rearview mirror.

"You age me, Boo," he says. That's his pet name for

me, Boo, because my big, wide-open brown eyes make me look permanently startled. "I got my first gray hair the day you were born. If I hadn't been there to see you come into the world with my own eyes, I'd swear the devil switched babies with us and gave us a little screaming demon."

He glances over at Mom with a weak smile, but she's not playing along.

So we go back to gloom and doom.

Dad was just getting off work when he picked us up for the doctor's appointment, so he's still in his police uniform. He's a constable here in Edgewood.

The Edge is a small town on Canada's west coast. The Rain Coast. From autumn to spring we get about eight months of wet weather. And even when the sun does break through, all we see is liquid sunshine.

Right now the downpour is drumming on the roof of the car. During the rainy season you tune out the constant *drip-drip-drip*ping—that never-ending background of white noise—the way you forget the sound of your own breathing.

The windows in back are all steamed up. I wipe a patch clear as we pull off the coast highway onto the road that runs along the ridge above town.

Edgewood is spread out below us. Not much to see now after dark, unless you can read the constellations of streetlights. They map out the neighborhoods, with a bright cluster in what passes for downtown, scattered sparks farther out in the hills and a curving line marking the seawall. Past that I catch the bobbing glimmers of boats tied up at the docks.

I'm trying to spot where our house is in this galaxy, but right now the trees block my view as the woods swallow us up.

The Edge is surrounded by ancient forest, giant century-old evergreens. The town was carved out of their turf. And the way they tower over you, leaning in together to eat up the light, it's like they're plotting to take it back.

We pass a sign that says BLIND CURVE AHEAD, and I know exactly where we are. Through the windshield I see a familiar stretch of road.

And I get a little shiver. Like they say, as if someone's stepping on my grave.

This is where they found me on a drizzly night last month, walking blindly down the centerline.

4

I started sleepwalking after my brain injury.

At first I just wandered around the house in the dark. Harmless.

Until I escaped one night and woke up standing outside, in the rainy dark. The cold hit me like a slap. I was soaking wet.

What is this? Where am I?

Looking down, I saw asphalt under my bare feet, and a painted white line.

I was in the middle of a road.

There was a light coming from behind me. And a voice calling.

"Jane?"

I spun around. Caught in the glare of headlights, I stumbled backward, holding my breath, bracing to get hit.

"Jane." That voice again, familiar. "Calm down. It's okay."

Shielding my eyes, I made out who it was.

Constable Granger. Dad's boss, standing beside his

squad car with the roof light flashing red and white. "What're you doing out here? Are you hurt?"

I could only shake my head, shocked speechless and trembling.

Looking down at myself, I suddenly realized I was wearing next to nothing. Just what I went to bed in: a long, ratty old T-shirt that stuck to me now like a second skin. And you could see right through it to my underwear with the little red hearts.

I crossed my arms to cover up my chest, wanting to die right there. Total unsurvivable embarrassment. But before I lost it and started crying, I squeezed my eyes shut and tried the old trick Dad taught me.

Bulletproof heart, he calls it. When I was little and the kids at school were bugging and bullying me, he showed me the Kevlar vest he wears on duty. "This is my armor," he said. "Keeps me safe when I'm out there. You need to grow your own armor, on the inside. Make your heart bulletproof."

So I forced myself to take a slow, deep breath.

Bulletproof. Then I opened my eyes and found my voice.

"Guess I got lost on my way to the bathroom." Sounding crazy, I know, but in control.

He looked at me like I was speaking Martian, then took off his rain slicker.

"Here. Cover up. Come on now, I'll drive you home."

Granger didn't ask any more questions on the way. The whole town knows my story.

Another time I escaped, Mom caught me while I was still in the driveway. She steered me safely back inside.

It's freaky and frightening to totally lose control over what your sleeping brain is getting you into. Makes you paranoid to take a nap, in case you wake up staring into the headlights of an oncoming truck. Because that wasn't the only time they tracked me down wandering along the same road out of town.

My late-night strolls were giving us all sleepless nights.

Everybody has a theory about why I'm doing it. Dad thinks it's some kind of death wish. Mom worries I want to run away. The doctors think it's a symptom of my injury.

I tried to cure my nightwalking by wedging a door-stop under my bedroom door. I even got Dad to put a lock on it so I could seal myself in. But my dozing brain just kicked the doorstop out of the way and opened the lock.

Dad finally came up with a solution. He gave me a ring. A plain silver band with a microchip embedded in it, a GPS locator chip.

It's the same technology they use to keep tabs on crooks on probation or under house arrest who have to wear ankle monitors. They have these alert systems in nursing homes and maternity wards too, in case some old-timer wanders off or somebody tries to steal a baby.

Now I wear my magic ring to bed. And if I get ten feet from the house an alarm gets sent to Dad's cell phone so he can go capture me. It's worked a few times already. I never make it to the end of the driveway before he catches up.

Now I don't have to worry about where I'm going to wake up anymore.

My sleep is under house arrest.

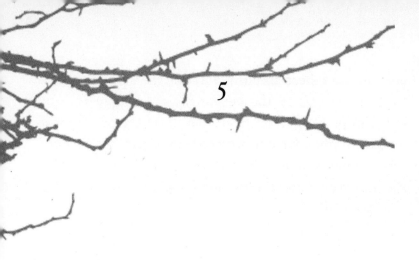

5

My phone rings at midnight, so I know it's Lexi. I told her to wait till later to call, to give me time if I needed to squeeze in a panic attack after my doctor's appointment.

"What's the verdict?" she says, no hello or anything. "You going under the knife?"

"Not yet. They want to wait."

"Wait for what? Do they think you're just going to sneeze that nail out one of these days? Or scoop it out with a Q-tip?"

I smile, lying back on my bed. Me and Lexi, we get each other. No heavy gloom-and-doom crap.

"They showed me on the X-ray. It's in there pretty deep. Digging it out could be more dangerous than leaving it for now."

I run my fingers over the shaved patch behind my left ear. I can feel the stubbly fuzz of new hair and the little dent in my skull where the nail entered. I was too far gone for the doctors to even try taking it out right away. Too risky, with me flatlining. So they stopped the bleeding, got my heart beating again and put the surgery off till later.

"You should get a copy of that X-ray. We could put it online. You'd be famous. 'Nailed Girl Cheats the Reaper.' Or, how about 'The Girl with Nine Lives'? We'd get you on the Discovery Channel or something."

"No thanks."

"How many lives have you got left, anyway?" she asks.

Getting nailed was just my latest close call.

"I must be on my last one now."

"I read about this girl," Lexi says, "who didn't even know she had a sewing needle stuck in her brain till she went to the doctor, after six months of headaches. She worked in a sweatshop where the needle snapped out of the machine and went right through the edge of her eye socket. She felt the jab but didn't realize it had penetrated. True story."

"Great. Maybe me and her can start our own freak show."

"So did the doctors clear you for school?"

"Unfortunately, yes." I've been off for two months, recovering. "They say I'm good to go. No danger signs. No bleeding, fevers, swelling or anything."

"So I'll drive by tomorrow morning and pick you up?"

"Sure. How bad is it at school? Should I be worried?"

"Well, they were calling you Psycho Jane for a while. But that was getting kind of old, so they've been trying out some new material."

"Like what?" I hate to ask.

"I heard Zombie Slut. You know, because you're back

from the dead. That's getting some play. And Reaper Creeper, which is pretty catchy. And what else . . . ?"

"Enough," I groan. "Don't ruin the surprise."

"I was thinking of something more like Lady Lazarus. If you go with that, we could start an online ministry and get donations. Maybe sell miracle springwater straight from your kitchen tap."

I shake my head. If I don't cut her off, she'll go on like this till dawn. Lexi's a major insomniac. She's so naturally wired, it's hard for her to sleep. She can't get her mind to shut down or her thoughts to shut up.

But it's been a long, long day and I'm ready to crash, so I give her a hint by yawning loudly.

"Okay," she says. "I hear you. Just called for the update. Sweet dreams, then. And hey, no playing in traffic tonight."

"I'll try."

After I hang up, I double-check the lock on my door. Dad's thinking of putting an alarm on it, but that might be a major hassle when I get up to pee at night. I drag my desk chair over to block the way, figuring if I bump into it that might wake me.

The rain gusts up against my window, tapping on the glass like a cat wanting in.

Before I turn out the light, I look around at the guys on my walls. Posters and photos from movies and magazines, showing a lot of skin. My dream guys: actors, musicians and models. My room is wallpapered in male flesh. Lexi says it's an overdose of lust.

But that's nothing compared to what's hidden away in

my closet. Okay, don't laugh—I'm addicted to romance novels. They're stacked floor to ceiling in there. I'm a sucker for doomed and dangerous love, reckless and crazy obsessions.

Lexi always makes fun of them. Mom looks at the covers and gets the giggles. Everybody laughs, so I hide my stash. My guilty pleasure. I'm a love junkie.

I kill the light, slip on my magic ring and get under the sheets.

Just when I'm dozing off, lying curled up on my side, I feel a little shiver down my spine. As if a draft has snuck into my room, or one of my dream guys has come in from the cold to spoon with me.

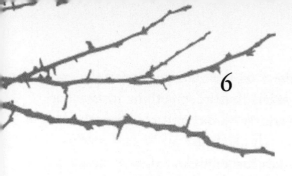

6

It started with my difficult birth. Mom nearly died having me. When they finally dragged me out into the world I was limp and lifeless, born without a pulse. They had to shock my tiny heart into beating.

Born dead. That set the mood for everything later.

So far I've survived poisoning, electrocution, a close encounter with a train and now this nail.

Don't get me wrong. I was never trying to hurt myself. This stuff just happened.

Stuff like—

At eight years old I was digging around in the kitchen cupboards, looking for art supplies for a project. But instead of paintbrushes and glue I found a plastic bottle with a skull and crossbones on the label, just like the one on pirate flags.

Later, I told Mom I thought the skull and bones meant it was a drink for pirates. Such a liar—I knew what the warning meant.

But I couldn't tell her the real reason why I drank the drain cleaner. Because I didn't know why.

But as I knelt there on the floor in front of the open cupboard, looking at that bottle, something strange happened. A wave of dizziness hit me. And a horrible shudder ran through me that felt like bugs crawling all over me. I heard this buzzing inside my head, as if some angry bee was trapped in there.

Then I thought my eyes were playing tricks, because my shadow started moving without me.

I watched, perfectly still, as the shadow of my left hand reached toward the bottle. Like a puppet on a string, I felt a tug and my hand followed the shadow, grabbing the bottle and taking it out.

There was a hazy dream feel to everything, smothering my fear and confusion.

I was watching myself taking directions from my shadow hands, opening the bottle. The liquid cleaner had a sharp, chemical smell.

Looking at my shadow on the floor, I could almost sense it staring back at me, making me do this. I couldn't help it. Lifting the bottle to my mouth, I started drinking.

It burned real bad and made my eyes tear up, but I managed to swallow half of the container and was starting to gag when Mom found me.

She screamed my name and knocked the bottle out of my hand. Then she stuck her fingers down my throat to make me throw up, and I spewed a puddle of chemical puke onto the kitchen floor.

I knelt there, breathless, dry-heaving till there was nothing left. Then we raced to the hospital.

Why? Mom kept asking me. Why did I do that?

How could I tell her it wasn't me? Shocked and shaken, I couldn't believe it myself.

For a long time after, I was literally scared of my own shadow. But eventually I convinced myself I'd imagined it—seeing things, like having a dream when I was awake.

Why did I do it? Who knows?

But there was nothing to be scared of. My shadow couldn't hurt me.

Could it?

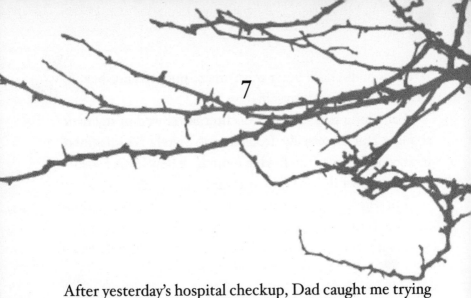

7

After yesterday's hospital checkup, Dad caught me trying to break out in my sleep last night. He says I got pushy this time, shoving him out of the way before I woke up with a heart-stopping shock on the front lawn.

So I have more drama to share with my therapist after school today.

At breakfast I'm groggy and grouchy, ready to pick a fight as Mom sets a paper cup in front of me: my morning pills. I'm still on antibiotics to ward off infection, anticonvulsants in case my brain gives me a seizure, a steroid to prevent swelling and others I don't even know what for.

"It's like you're feeding me the whole pharmacy."

"Don't be a grumpy patient," she says. "Come on now. Down the hatch with them."

She watches me swallow the pills.

"How's your head feeling, Boo?" Dad asks, sipping his coffee. "Any more migraines?"

That little nail missed all the vital areas—a one-in-a-million shot, the doctors say—but it can still hurt like a bitch sometimes. "My head's a mess. But no pain or anything for the last couple of days."

Just looking at Dad's face, you can tell *he's* no stranger to pain. His nose has been broken so many times it's kind of squashed, with the bridge dented in. His left eyebrow is a zigzag from where it was split and didn't get sewn back straight. Souvenirs from his boxing days.

But all that damage is from before he met Mom. Back when he was known around town as *Bulldog*. Mom housebroke him a long time ago. She says now he's only like a bulldog on the outside—inside he's a pussycat.

She puts a plate of French toast in front of me and leans in to press the back of her hand against my forehead.

I sigh. "No fever, Mom. Quit worrying."

She takes her hand away. "Quit worrying me, then."

We scowl at each other. I got my looks from her, but where she's pretty, I'm just odd. My mouth is too wide, my eyes way too big. We're both blond, but her hair is soft and wavy, a honey shade, while mine is a frizzy, straw-colored tangle. Mom says I'll grow into my looks, just like she says my curves will come. But when? I'm seventeen and I still can't fake any real cleavage. And where's my ass? Seriously, I'm sitting on bone here.

I notice Mom and Dad watching me across the table. I catch them doing that a lot lately. Like they think I'm going to vanish any second.

"Where's your ring?" she asks.

I shrug. "I'm not gonna wear that thing all day."

"Why not?"

"What, so you can track every step I take?"

"We're not spying on you," she says. "We just want to make sure you're safe."

"I'm safe enough," I grumble. "Besides, I only get lost at night, when I'm asleep."

If it was up to her I'd be under twenty-four-hour surveillance.

"Why do you have to make it into such a huge thing?" she asks.

I take an angry bite of my toast. Can't blame her for worrying, really. But I don't need that ring on my finger every second, reminding me what a wreck I am. How I can't be trusted—can't even trust myself.

Mom's waiting for an answer. Our stare-down is broken by a car horn sounding from the driveway. Lexi saves the day.

"That's my ride," I say. "Gotta go. Gonna be late."

"Hold on," she tells me. "We're not done here."

"Dad?" I turn to the law. "Am I under arrest?"

The constable looks between me and Mom. "You're free to go, I guess. For now. But just think about it, okay? And don't leave town."

Mom frowns at him, shaking her head.

I stuff the last of the toast into my mouth and make my escape, rushing out into the gray January drizzle.

"Perfect timing," I tell Lexi, getting in her car.

As we pull away from the curb and head for school, she glances over. "You look wasted. Rough night?"

"I went sleepwalking again, but my dad stopped me from escaping."

I reach for the rearview mirror and twist it around to see myself. My hair's snarled, a wild jungle of a mane. I try pressing it down, but it just springs back. At least it distracts from the circles under my eyes.

"I look like roadkill."

Beside me, Lexi looks less like the Reaper's little sister today and more like a naughty ninja. Her everyday uniform is black leather jacket over long-sleeved shirt, miniskirt, knee-high socks and chunky-heeled shoes that boost her two inches. She's a shorty, but she's got bite.

Her look says, You can't handle this, get lost and dream on. I could never make that work. My look just says Help!

"Speaking of roadkill," I say, giving up on my hair. "Has my sleepwalking gone viral? Does everybody know?"

Lexi nods. "Face it, girl. You're notorious. They're saying you run the streets naked after midnight, howling at the moon, feasting on human flesh."

She gives me a half smile to show she's half joking.

"Great," I say. "All these years with me trying so hard to be normal, and now . . ."

"Well, it's good to have you back. I was getting lonely being the only freak in class. The *Creep Sisters* ride again."

That's what they call us at school, a name that's stuck to us since sixth grade.

Lexi says we were best friends before we even met. Like it was destiny that brought us together that first time in the school washroom.

Back then I was recovering from another close call. I had to wear gloves everywhere because my hands were still healing.

Lexi was the new girl, showing up in the middle of the school year.

She was standing at the mirrors when I came out of the washroom stall that afternoon. I tried not to stare. Nobody knew anything about her—where she was from, why she dressed all in black and went around filming weird stuff with her cell phone, like a dead seagull she found on the soccer field or some workers feeding branches into a wood chipper.

Hard not to stare at the mystery girl. I loved her hair, so silky black and straight.

I flinched when I saw she was looking back at me in the mirror.

"I've been watching you," she said.

"Huh?" I felt like I'd been caught, but caught doing what, I didn't know. Her dark eyes were locked on me.

"What's with the gloves? You cold?"

"No." I put my hands behind my back.

"Are you scared of germs or something?"

I shook my head.

"So why are you wearing them? What are you hiding? Can I see?"

"What? No. Why?"

The new girl was moving in fast-forward, leaving me kind of dazed. I'd come there to pee, not to get interrogated.

"Whatever it is," she said, "I'll bet you I got it beat."

I glanced from her to the door, thinking of making a quick escape. But this human question mark with the silky hair had me hooked. "Beat how?"

"I got something more freaky. Let's do a show-and-tell. Then we'll see who wins for the weirdest."

"Is it something gross?"

"More like bizzare."

I shrugged. "You go first."

"Okay." She bent and took off her right shoe and sock, till she was standing there with one bare foot. "Check it out."

I looked down. It was a normal foot, except for the big toe.

"It's blue," I said. "What happened?"

"Spider bite."

"No way."

She nodded. "A little wolf spider. It bit me when I stepped on it by accident. You should have seen my foot, it swelled up like a balloon. And when it shrank back down again, all the toes were blue."

"Why?"

"They weren't getting enough blood. So you know what the doctor did? He stuck blood-sucking leeches on my toes, to get more blood to flow into them."

"Leeches?" I cringed.

"Yeah. Little black vampire slugs. And it worked. Now it's just the big toe that's blue. Still working on that one."

She wiggled it at me. "So what do you think? I'm pretty freaky, huh?"

"Yeah," I blurted out. "I mean no. Not you, just your toe."

Then she laughed. It was the first time I'd seen her look anything but dead serious. So I smiled too.

"It's your turn," she said. "What are you hiding?"

There was no turning back now.

"It's kind of gross," I warned her. Then I pulled the gloves off and let her see my hands.

I waited for shock or disgust. She leaned in for a closer look.

"Cool," she said finally. "How did you do that?"

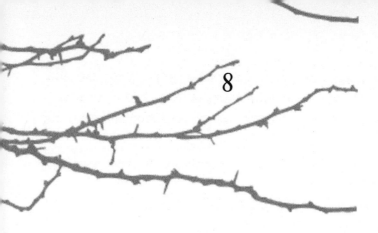

8

After the close call when I hurt my hands, I became small-town famous for a while.

It started with a wicked windstorm blasting Edge-wood.

Hurricane-force gales kept me up all night, shaking the walls of our house and howling like demons. It felt as if the whole place was going to get torn up and tossed into the sky, like Dorothy's house in *The Wizard of Oz*.

When the storm finally blew itself out, the geography of our neighborhood had changed. Trees uprooted, the street buried in debris. I was stunned when I stumbled out into that strange new world that morning, stepping over a twisted metal pretzel that used to be a lawn chair.

The big oak in our front yard had crashed over, taking down the power lines with it. A thick black live wire was whipping across our driveway like an angry snake.

The way it twisted, coiling and lashing out, was hypnotic. I was standing in the litter of leaves and splintered branches on the lawn, staring at it, when I felt suddenly dizzy. For a moment it seemed as if the wind was blowing right through me. There was a strong buzz in my ears, like I'd stumbled on a hive of hornets. And I felt the weirdest sensation, as if something was wriggling and writhing over my skin.

Then I caught sight of something moving down by my boots.

I was about to step away when I saw that it was just my shadow. So I stayed still.

But it didn't.

The shadow of my left rain boot stretched out and stepped forward.

That was when my brain shut down and something else took over. My shadow was a magnet, dragging me along, leading me onto the driveway toward the power line, which was spitting sparks into the air—high-voltage venom.

But now I wasn't scared. I watched all this play out, a spectator in my own head.

The sparks were raining down around me. I crouched, and my shadow hands reached out, my real ones following after them. The charged air lifted the hairs on my arms.

The wire snapped out blindly, as if searching for contact.

Then it struck my hands.

An explosion of cold fire blasted through me, freezing me rigid for a long second. Then I was flying, thrown back. I hit the garage door and crumpled to the ground.

My heart forgot to beat. I hurt everywhere. Every inch and atom of me.

I lay there with my cheek pressed to the pavement.

My eyes were still working. Before I blacked out, I saw a pair of shadow boots standing beside me. My stare was locked straight ahead, couldn't look up. The boots were black silhouettes cut from the bright morning air.

I could feel my legs jerking convulsively, trying to get me up and running away from this dark thing.

I thought if it touched me I'd fall through that black hole shaped like my shadow. It would swallow me.

My vision started to die off, flickering in and out. And with every fading glimpse, those boots seemed closer.

Ten thousand volts, the doctors told me. That was the shock I took when I touched the live power line. Should be dead—they didn't say it, but I knew what they were thinking.

My fingers were burned badly, scabby and peeling for weeks. The nails turned black and fell off. I had to wear the gloves, not just to hide my hideousness but to keep my hands safe from infection. My ears rang with an annoying mosquito buzz off and on for months, driving me crazy.

I told Mom and Dad I didn't see the fallen line till it was too late. Like it snuck up on me.

Why couldn't I tell them the real story? Because it was so impossibly crazy. I didn't want to believe it—that my shadow could turn on me. I'd buried the memory of my earlier poisoning so deep it had the feel of a strange dream. This brought it all back.

Denial is a powerful thing. I told myself the electrocution had messed with my mind, knocking me out and making me remember things wrong. I hadn't seen what I'd thought I was seeing.

Still, one night when Mom was tucking me in, I asked her: "Does my shadow have a life of its own?"

She laughed. "Your shadow is stitched to your feet. Can't make a move without you."

But what if mine had come unstitched somehow? What would it try next?

9

Everybody in the cafeteria is watching.

"What's with all the staring?" I ask Lexi. "Are they expecting me to put on a show? Do a trick?"

"Get used to it, you're a celebrity. A living, breathing magic trick. You danced with death, wrestled with the Reaper. And won."

Makes it hard to eat when every chew, slurp and swallow is under observation. I've spent ten minutes trying to finish this apple.

"Watch out," Lexi tells me. "Idiots incoming."

Two smirking loser guys are heading toward us. I brace myself, putting on my armor inside. Making my heart bulletproof.

"Hey, Jane," says loser number one. "Heard you got nailed. Try getting screwed next time. Might put a smile on your face."

Number two snorts a laugh.

"Yawn," Lexi says. "Seriously, that's the best you and your boyfriend could come up with?" She holds up her cell phone and snaps a photo of them.

"What's that for?" asks number one. "You need something to keep you warm and wet at night?"

"No. There's an online support group for virgins. I'll add your profiles. Thank me later. Bye, now."

She gives them a little wave. They leave, muttering "bitch" and "skank" under their breath.

Lexi rolls her dark eyes at me. "Didn't you miss all this?"

I sigh. "Feels like I'm on display at the zoo, where they're going to take turns rattling my cage."

Out of the corner of my eye, I notice someone coming up beside our table. But this idiot isn't here for me.

It's Max. Lexi's ex, who won't stay ex'ed.

"Hey, Lexi. You're looking delicious."

A quick sketch of him: Messy black hair. Smoky gray eyes. Killer long lashes. Looks like he was raised by wolves. He plays in his own crappy little garage band. And he's a total slut. He cheated on Lexi every chance he got.

"What do you want?" she says.

"Just to talk, or text. You never answer me anymore."

"That's because it's over."

She keeps her eyes down, like she's checking out her nail polish. Lexi can't look at Max. The breakup is fresh and raw. Hurts too much.

"Come on," he says. "We don't have to be enemies. We can still do the video stuff, right?"

Lexi makes these short films she posts online, and she got Max to do the music on a couple of them. In exchange, she shot a video for his band last year and made them look like they were for real.

"We can't do anything," she says.

He runs his fingers through his hair, messing it some more, and tries his best wolf smile. "How about with that new film you were working on? I already made up a little mood music for it." She's shaking her head, but that's not stopping him. "Don't say no till you hear it."

"I don't want to hear it. Don't want to hear you."

I know how tough this is for her, so I jump in.

"Why don't you just go." I wave him off.

He glares at me. We had a mutual hate thing going from the start. I knew he was bad for her—toxic. And he thinks I'm the reason she broke up with him.

"Heard you were dead." His gray eyes go cold.

"I was. It didn't stick."

"Try harder next time."

Then he exits.

"What a scumbag," I say to Lexi. "But you were great. Strong. You didn't give in."

It was rough helping her break her addiction to Max, because he really knew how to play her. Whenever she tried to pull away he understood just what to say, and she kept falling for him. But no more.

"School's like a recurring nightmare," she says. "Where all your mistakes come back to haunt you."

I nod, thinking about that last thing he said.

"What did that mean, anyway—'Try harder next time'?"

She shrugs. "He was being an ass."

"Yeah, but is that what everybody's saying? That I tried to kill myself? I mean, they're all supposed to think it was just an unintentional clumsy freak thing that happened. That's the official story."

"I know. But suicide by nail gun makes a juicier story. They're going with that instead."

So that's what's behind all the staring and whispers. Makes me want to scream, It's not my fault! I didn't do this to myself! It's not me.

Putting my half-eaten apple down, I notice the shadow of my hand on the tabletop. Matching my movements. Following my lead.

For now.

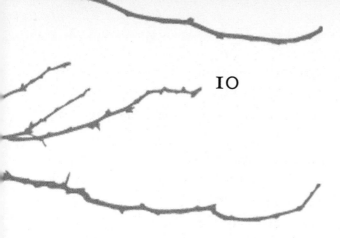

10

Once a week I have to go see Dr. Iris, psychiatrist.

I tried to argue my way out of this, saying I was just accident-prone and clumsy, not depressed, screwy or suicidal. But Dad wasn't buying it. He's a natural lie detector. And my explanation for how I got this nail in my head sounded suspicious even to me.

"You need a professional you can talk to," he said. "To help you work things out."

The problem with my "things" is that they're impossible. I'd come close to telling Dad the truth before, but I always pulled back. He only believes in what he can see with his own eyes, what he can lay his hands on. No way he could wrap his mind around what's been happening to me. And after all the crap I've put Mom through, I didn't want to add having a mentally disturbed daughter to her worries.

If I spilled my secret they'd lock me up. And I don't blame them—if I wasn't me, I wouldn't believe me.

So I lie.

"Getting back to normal?" Dr. Iris asks me now.

"I guess." Whatever that is.

She has mousy brown hair pulled back and tied up. Pale skin. Thick-framed glasses. Dressed all in gray, a light sweater over a blouse, knee-length skirt and tights.

"How have you been sleeping?"

"I fall asleep okay. It's just staying there—you know, in bed, in the house—that's hard."

"How often do you sleepwalk?"

"Maybe three times a week. But they've got this alarm system set up to keep track of me. So I can't really escape."

I can't help fidgeting when I'm here, nervously playing with my hair, finding endless tangles.

"How do these disturbances make you feel?"

"I don't know. Helpless, I guess. Out of control."

I try not to relax, scared to let down my guard. I've got too much to hide. Her office is designed to calm you and open you up—from the warm pastel colors to the slightly dimmed lighting, the soft comfy chairs and even the way she sits there with her legs tucked under like we're friends chatting.

"And when you're awake, you're in control?" she asks.

"Yeah. Of course."

Except when my shadow takes over—if only I could say.

"And you're back in school?"

I nod. "First day."

"How was it?"

I shrug, finding a new snarl in my hair. "Same old crap, but worse."

She raises her eyebrows, waiting for more.

"Everybody's spreading lies about me."

"What kind of lies?"

I hesitate. There's one subject I avoid here, even though it's always hanging in the air between us, like a bad smell. But there's no way out now.

"They're saying it was a suicide attempt."

I watch her closely to see if she's thinking the same thing, but she's giving nothing away.

"What's it like, hearing that?"

"Pisses me off. Like they think they know me. Like they know anything." I squirm around on the chair, sneaking a peek at my watch. I've still got a lot of time to kill here. "People are always shooting off their mouths about me."

"Because of your previous incidents?"

"Yeah. You know how it is—small town with small minds. And big mouths."

"What do they say?"

"That I've got some kind of death wish. That I'm crazy."

I shake my head, looking away from the doctor to the rain-washed windows.

But I'm not crazy. How can I be so sure? After all that's happened to me?

Because there was one time that my shadow turned on me when I wasn't alone.

I had a witness.

Lexi.

II

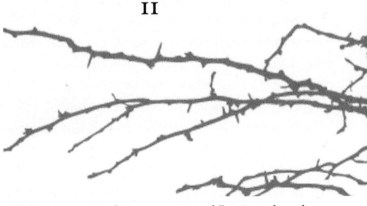

The summer we were thirteen, me and Lexi took a short-cut to her place on the outer limits of Edgewood. Quick-est way there is to follow the train tracks that run past town.

Summer is a real shock to the system around here. After months of endless downpours and gray skies, the sun breaks through like a miracle. We stumble out into the light, as if waking up from the longest dream.

So on this hot June afternoon, I was walking on the tracks, using one of the steel rails like a balance beam, with my arms held out to keep me steady. There was a warm breeze, carrying the smell of everything green.

Lexi was up ahead, searching by the side of the tracks for flattened pennies. Kids line them up on the rails for the trains to crush. They're supposed to be good luck after. But when the steel wheels hit them, the coins go flying, so you never find them all.

"Got one," she called out, the copper flashing in the sun as she held it up. "An American penny. Lincoln's head is all weird now. He looks like an alien."

"Find me one. I could use some luck."

I was scaring up crickets as I went, stepping over a few sunning themselves on the rails, sending them hopping into the weeds.

My focus was on my feet when Lexi shouted.

"Train!"

The tracks made a sharp turn up ahead into the trees, so the train was still out of sight.

A humming drone filled my ears, as if the crickets were starting a riot. Then I felt a vibration shoot through me that I thought was rising up from the rail underfoot.

I went to step off the tracks. But my feet stayed stuck. Looking down, I couldn't see what was holding them. But they wouldn't budge. It was like they were magnetized to the rail.

With the sun behind me, my shadow stretched ahead across the wooden planks. Just as my confusion started to edge into panic, I felt that familiar haziness.

The vibration got stronger, making me tremble all over as if something was squirming over my flesh. My shadow was taking over. This time it didn't need to make me do anything but stand still. And wait.

No! I screamed inside. I won't let you! Not again!

I wanted to reach down and pull my feet free, but my arms were paralyzed at my sides. Useless. I saw my shadow shift. The silhouette of my head seemed to turn around to face me.

As the deadening calm swept over me, I heard Lexi calling my name. Her voice was like a lifeline, keeping me from going under.

The train broke from the trees, speeding straight for me. Lexi was yelling.

"Move, Jane! Get off!"

But my feet were welded in place.

"Jane!"

I leaned to my left, straining to fall over, out of the train's path. Muscle pulling against muscle. It felt like they might tear before giving way.

I was tilting. But too slowly! The train was heartbeats away.

"Jane!"

The roar of the engine was closing in. I was screaming in my head—

Let! Me! Go!

Something snapped in me. A blinding flare spiked through my brain.

And I fell.

Seemed like slow motion. In that moment I caught sight of my shadow still lying on the tracks. Not moving with me.

Then I hit the ground hard, the breath knocked out of me. The train whipped by with a blast of wind and the screech of its whistle.

I lay gasping as it blurred past within arm's reach. It went on forever, car after car. Lexi was out of sight on the other side.

The end of the train zipped by with a gust of hot, dusty air, making me cough.

Then Lexi was there, leaning over me.

"You okay, Jane? What happened? You get stuck?"

But I wasn't looking at her. My eyes were focused on the tracks beside me. Because something was moving.

My shadow slid over the steel rail, black as liquid tar.

Frozen in place, too shocked to even try to get away, I watched as it got closer and closer. One of its hands stretched out to me. And I felt my own hand tremble as if it wanted to reach for it.

"What—?" Lexi was saying. "What is that?"

When those dark fingers touched mine, it was like my shadow slipped right into me. As if I was a sponge soaking it up. It sent an electric rush through my body, squeezing my heart tight for a few seconds, before fading so I could breathe again.

"Jane! You okay? Say something."

I had to force some air into my lungs before I could speak. "Did you . . . see it?"

"What was that?"

"My . . . shadow."

She frowned down at me. "What do you mean? I don't—"

"You saw . . . what it did?"

She was shaking her head. "I don't know what I just saw. It's like some weird trick of the light. Maybe the clouds blocking—"

"No clouds." We looked up at the clear blue sky.

And we sat there by the tracks for a long time while the sun melted away the freeze inside me.

Time to catch my breath. And tell Lexi my secret.

* * *

Following my close call with the train, me and Lexi searched everywhere, online and off, to see if anything like this had ever happened to anybody else. I found out I was alone in my strangeness. A million times I asked myself, Why me?

For a while I wondered if it had something to do with how I was born. Maybe it took the doctors too long to get my heart beating back then and I got damaged somehow. Not in my brain or body, but deeper—some kind of soul damage. Crazy, I know. But I wondered.

If Lexi hadn't been there to keep me from falling totally under my shadow's spell, I wouldn't have been able to pull away like I did.

Anyway, after that my killer shadow seemed to give up. Years went by with no more drama. The shade I cast didn't make a move without me. So my fears faded, and I even started to think maybe I had just dreamed it up. That me and Lexi shared a little hallucination back there by the tracks.

Some kids have imaginary friends, maybe I had an imaginary assassin.

I was wrong.

12

After school I stick around for the premiere of Lexi's latest cinematic masterpiece. Her film club meets in the theater arts room. She likes putting her short flicks online, but sometimes she says it's good to have a live audience, even when they're brutal and criticize her stuff.

I take a seat at the back. The lights are dim, and the show has already started. But it's not Lexi's turn yet.

On the big-screen TV up front there's a close-up of a pair of ballet shoes. The camera pulls back so we see a crying girl looking down at them. I recognize the girl from my English lit class. She pulls out a can of lighter fluid and soaks the shoes, strikes a match and drops it on them. The camera zooms in as they burst into flames, and stays with the shot for a long moment before the whole thing fades to black.

Mr. Steiner, the drama teacher, gets up.

"Good stuff, Valerie. Nice use of montage, and smooth editing. Any comments?" He opens it up to the group.

I spot Lexi on the far side and give her a little wave. She mouths to me, I'm next.

"Why did she burn the shoes?" some guy asks.

Valerie tells him, "Because she was never going to be good enough."

Other comments range from critical—"What a drama queen"—to confused—"What does 'montage' mean again?"

Then Mr. Steiner cues up the next flick.

A LEXI CRANE FILM flashes on the screen.

Followed by the title: *THE END OF THE ROAD*. White letters fading away into a black background.

Then a pair of eyes fills the screen. Frog eyes, green flecked with yellow, vertical slits for pupils. They blink, and the camera pulls back so you see the whole frog and the wet pavement under him. His throat pulsates as he croaks. As the camera zooms out even farther, you find he's not alone. There's a crowd of frogs on the rainy asphalt.

The view cuts to black again and the caption:

EVERY SPRING THEY COME.

A wide shot shows a stretch of road that's alive with the hopping mob of amphibians. There's a chorus of croaking now.

TO CROSS OVER.

A car roars past, speeding through them. Squashing some.

TO FIND THEIR MATING GROUNDS.

A low-level shot gives the frog's point of view. The forest is on the far side, with the wetlands hidden there. But standing between them and their destination is the blur of giant wheels passing by.

SOME MAKE IT.

The lucky ones move off the pavement and gravel shoulder toward the safety of the trees.

OTHERS DON'T.

The broken and flattened seem to outnumber the living. But they keep coming, wave after wave of them.

SOME FIND A NEW BEGINNING.

The view cuts to a swampy pond filled with frogs hooking up. Then a close-up of little black tadpoles swimming through green algae.

OTHERS FIND THE END OF THE ROAD.

The camera picks out one victim lying belly-up on the asphalt, eyes shut, legs limp. The croaking quiets down to silence. The image freezes for a long moment before going to black.

Mr. Steiner gets up again.

"Beautifully strange, as always, Lexi. Morbidly moving. Nice choice of camera angles. Great sound quality. Okay, discussion. What are your thoughts?"

Lexi said this is where they all tear her flicks apart.

"What did that mean?"

"I don't get it."

"There's nothing to get."

"It's froggy porn."

"That was so gross."

"Why does she always have to do dead stuff?"

Lexi stares straight ahead at the blank screen, a hint of a smile at the corner of her mouth. For her, these critics are just indie-film wannabes who have never had an original idea in their lives. But she keeps coming because Steiner is good with the technical stuff.

A new voice breaks in. "It's brilliant."

Searching for who said that, I see Max slouched in a chair on the far side of the room.

"Brilliant how?" asks Valerie.

He shrugs. "There were lots of metaphors and stuff. About life and death. Makes you think."

Lexi doesn't look back, but I can tell she recognizes his voice by how she's got her eyes squeezed shut.

"More like makes you puke," Valerie says.

Mr. Steiner holds up his hands. "Try to keep it constructive."

After some tech talk about storyboarding and sound editing, the group breaks up.

I go over to Lexi before Max can move in. I give him the evil eye.

"Great stuff," I tell her. "Loved those low-angle shots from the frog's point of view."

I helped out months ago when she was shooting it, holding the umbrella over her and watching for cars.

"Is he still there?" she asks.

"Just leaving."

I watch him go. He chats up Valerie on the way out. Max is giving up for now, because he's got no shot at getting Lexi alone to try to play her.

"Okay, he's gone."

She lets out her breath. Lexi's got a weak spot when it comes to slick and shallow users like Max. He's kind of a drug to her. She feels this chemical attraction that blinds her to his sleaziness. She says she's over him, but it's hard to kick your own chemistry.

"So you liked it?" She packs up her stuff. "This is the first time you saw the final cut."

"You're a genius. A visionary. But I'm glad you left out those gory shots of the splattered and exploded bodies."

"Yeah, I thought that might be overkill. It's supposed to be a romance, after all."

"What?" I shake my head. "Lexi, I know romance. You're talking to a love junkie. How is getting squashed and smeared romantic? You ought to put a disclaimer at the end: *Lots of animals were killed making this movie.*"

"I know," she says. "But what could be more romantic? They died for love."

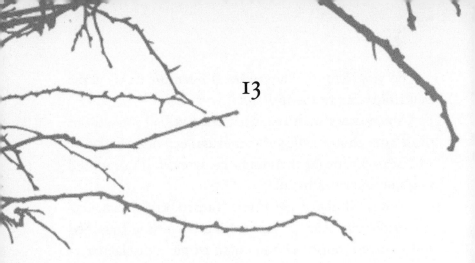

13

I suck the blood off my thumb before it drips on the roses.

"Careful," Mom says.

I'm helping out at her flower shop, the Blushing Rose, filling an order for a wedding tomorrow. Right now I'm dethorning three dozen white roses for the bouquets.

"You want to talk about last night?" she asks.

"What do you mean? What about it?"

"You went walking again."

"I did? I don't remember anything. I guess you caught me before I got too far?"

"After two blocks. You were moving fast. Sleep-jogging." She clips some stems, finishing up one of the centerpieces for the reception. "When I tried to guide you back, you took a swing at me."

"What?" I strain for any memory of this and come up blank. "I didn't actually hit you, did I?"

"No. It was a slow punch. Easy to duck."

"Wow, sorry. It's not me doing it. Really. I don't know where all that's coming from."

She adds a few carnations to the arrangement. "I was going to shake you awake right there. But they say that's bad for the sleeper, too much of a shock."

It's a real heart-stopper when that happens. Like being woken from the deepest sleep by a scream.

"I'm nothing but trouble," I say.

"Just remember to wear your ring to bed."

Poor Mom. I've been worrying her since birth. She almost died in labor, and couldn't have any more kids after me. *You're my one and only,* she always says. *My miracle.* I've never had the heart to tell her how defective her miracle is. How could I ever ask her to believe the impossible, the invisible, the insane?

I start tying the bouquets together with red ribbon.

"Ryan was asking for you," Mom says, out of nowhere.

My heart skips a beat. I can feel her watching for my reaction, so I focus on the roses.

"When was this?" I ask, snipping ribbon.

"Today. When he was making the morning delivery."

Ryan works at the Raincoast Greenhouse. It's the local supplier for hothouse flowers, fruits and veggies. He's my secret dream sex god. Tall, with wavy blond hair, blue-green eyes and a husky voice that melts my spine.

"What did he say?"

"Just hi. And he asked how you were doing. You know, when you were recovering in the hospital he brought flowers. That was really sweet."

She wants me to share. To bare my heart and chat about guys with her.

I shrug. "I guess."

"You can talk to me. About anything."

"I know," I say. But really, there's so much I can't tell her without sounding nuts.

Mom sighs, giving up for now.

As I snip thorns from the stems, my mind fixes on Ryan. My lord of lust. My doomed crush.

I met him last year when me and Mom drove out to the greenhouse. She brought me along to take pictures of the new floral varieties they were trying out. When she started talking rose hybrids with the owner, I wandered off.

The place felt like a jungle, the warm humidity a nice break from the frigid day outside. The air was so rich with oxygen, making everything seem more intense. The smells were dizzying; each breath I took hit me with a dozen different scents. I found the tropical flowers and was stunned by their wild explosions of color.

One variety caught my eye. On the top of their tall green-blue stalks grew flowers with long, spiky petals of bright orange, yellow, deep blue and violet. Like God used every crayon in the box on them. And they had the perfect name. I was zooming in to take a close-up shot when a voice out of nowhere made me jump.

"Bird-of-paradise."

Turning, I spotted Ryan coming around a corner in the jungle, pushing a wheelbarrow.

"They're my favorite," he said.

Ryan's eyes were what grabbed me first. Aqua-green, they seemed to reflect the surrounding colors.

"You can see why they call them that." He stopped beside me. "With the tip of the stalk pointing out like a beak, and the orange and yellow petals sticking up like feathers."

I saw the bird in them. If I unfocused my eyes a little I could imagine those brightly colored wings taking flight.

"Not shy with their colors," I said.

"In the wild they're pollinated by sunbirds who perch on the flower's beak so they can drink the nectar, getting their feet dusted with pollen."

I noticed a change in the air right then, from the intoxicating floral overdose to something rank and rotten.

"What is that smell?" I asked.

"Oh, sorry. That's me. My manure." He gestured to the full wheelbarrow. "Well, it's not *my* manure. It didn't come from me." He winced, hearing his words. "That didn't sound right."

I laughed. "No. Not really."

He started blushing. I felt my own skin warming too, as I stood next to this hot guy in the hothouse.

"Well, whose manure is it?" I said, teasing him.

"Comes from sheep. They make the best. Very rich. High in nitrogen, potash and other nutrients. And I'm sure that's more than you ever wanted to know about fertilizer. Why don't I wheel this away and let the air clear."

I watched him go, wishing he'd stay and tell me more—about sheep poo or anything else.

The bird-of-paradise became my favorite flower after

that. Ryan remembered too. There was a bunch waiting for me when I woke up in the hospital.

"What's that smile for?" Mom asks now, shaking me from my memory.

I shrug. "Just . . . daydreaming."

Of paradise.

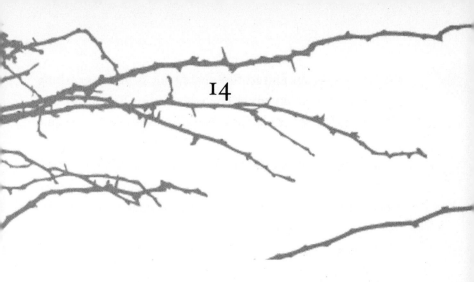

14

Lexi lives with her mother and grandmother on the far side of town. It's a little place that's too small to hold all their tempers, so Lexi moved into the room above the garage. It's not like they hate each other. There's a crazy kind of love between them, but it's flammable. One wrong spark and *boom!*

Right now I'm sitting in front of the computer at Lexi's desk, with her watching over my shoulder. She wants my review of the rough cut of her next short film.

It's another one of her mood pieces. It's called *Breaking Up,* and it stars a dead toad. In speeded up time-lapse footage we watch him decompose. There's a fast-forward feeding frenzy of hungry bugs, picking him clean. This image is edited together with close-up shots of things breaking: bottles, icicles and lightbulbs. Finally we freeze on the skeletonized toad. The screen fades to black, and it says *NOT THE END.* Because now the bony toad reappears, and the whole thing goes in reverse. He gets uneaten. In rewind, it's like the bugs are fixing him up and stitching his skin back together. While this is happening, the bottles, bulbs and icicles unshatter. When everything is back in one piece again, the screen goes black and says *THE BEGINNING*.

"So, what do you think?" Lexi asks.

I reach for my can of Coke and take a sip, to stall for time. Lexi says you can't always explain these mood pieces. They're like video poems, you have to feel them. Right now I'm feeling slightly nauseous.

"I think it's . . . hopeful," I say. "In a weird way."

"Hopeful how?"

"Well, everything gets fixed up, right? Like new again. It's the closest you've ever come to a happy ending."

"So you get it, then?" she asks.

I take another long sip. "Um. I think I do. Just so I'm clear on this—are you like the dead toad? Metaphorically, I mean. After your breakup with Max?"

Lexi nods. "You're the only one in the world who gets me."

"I guess one is better than none."

I notice a photo on the wall showing her monstrously swollen foot after her spider bite. Next to it is another shot with the leeches stuck on her toes to heal them.

I used to think it was because of me that Lexi got into all this dark and morbid stuff. But really, she was like that before we even met. It's what pulled her to me from the start, after hearing about my electrocution.

Her dad's the one who got her started on moviemaking. He was always shooting home videos. Those old movies, hours and hours of them, are all she has left of him. He took off when she was ten.

"But seriously," I tell her now. "You're a sick little monkey. You should be in therapy, not me."

"Well, we can share bunk beds over at the asylum." She smiles. "Speaking of crazy crap, has your shadow been behaving?"

"It hasn't tried anything since I got nailed." I hold my hand under the desk lamp, wiggling my fingers. Their shadows wiggle back, perfectly synchronized. "Maybe it's gone, whatever it was. Maybe it's over."

Wishful thinking, but sometimes that's all you've got.

These days my shadow only turns against me in my nightmares.

"Maybe," Lexi says, resting her hand on my shoulder. "Hey, get up. I want to play you something. Max emailed me the music he did for my rain project." She sees me shaking my head. "I know. I was going to hit Delete. And I'm not going to reply to him, or anything. But it can't hurt to hear it. I don't have to use it."

"I just don't want you relapsing after you've finally kicked your Max habit."

I remember the months of boyfriend rehab I went through with her.

"I'm cured. Really." Lexi sounds like she's trying to convince herself.

"What's your 'rain project' again?"

"It's called *A Thousand Words for Rain*. You know how we have so many names for it here on the coast, for all its moods. I've been shooting around town, on the beaches and trails."

As she brings up a new file on the computer I wander around her room. The walls are covered with photos she took before she came to Edgewood. Lots of sunny beach shots, palm trees and endless blue skies.

Lexi grew up in San Diego—the opposite of here. Going from hot, bright Southern California to the cool gray Raincoast was a serious shock for her.

When her dad hit the road, Lexi and her mom had to move here to live with her gran.

"Give this a listen." She turns up the volume.

Max's music fills the room. Soft acoustic-guitar stuff, kind of dreamy. That guy can play. The strumming builds to a boom of drums.

"Thunder," she calls over the music.

It goes quiet again with a whisper of brush on a snare drum, like drizzle gusting against a windowpane.

I can see why Lexi falls for the guys she does. Beautiful liars like Max. She hates it when I say this, but they're clones of her dad.

"Does this make you think *rain*?" she asks.

I nod.

As the drums boom again, they're echoed by real thunder outside. There's always another storm coming.

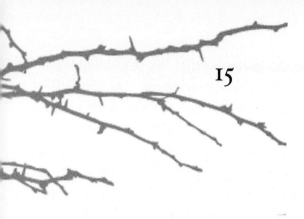

15

I wake slowly, with the sound of my name echoing in my ears. Someone's calling me. From far away.

Jane.

No. Let me sleep. Five more minutes, Mom.

Jane.

Whispered closer, tickling my ear. Not Mom's voice. More like a guy's.

Pulled from my doze, I try to open my eyes.

But they won't open! Must be sticky with too much mascara gunk and sleep sand. I start rubbing and feel something weird.

What is this?

Under my fingertips it feels like I've got false eyelashes stuck on, gluing my eyes shut. But I never wear those.

I try to pull whatever it is off, but it won't come loose.

It seems more like . . . thread?

Stitches!

As if my lids are sewn shut. No! I'm not thinking right. Still half-asleep.

Wake up!

I pluck at one thread, and it tugs the skin, stinging.

Get up! Go to the bathroom and wash this crap off!

I sit up in bed and my head cracks on something solid, just inches above me.

What's that?

My hands fumble blindly, find a flat surface looming over me. That can't be there. Where am I? I reach out, and my palms hit walls on both sides of me. Boxing me in. Like . . .

Like a coffin!

No. No! Get me out of here!

Must be dreaming.

I go to scream and wake up the house. But I can't.

My lips won't open either. Touching them, I feel more thread, more stitches. From one corner of my mouth to the other. So tight I have to breathe through my nose.

I scream anyway. It comes out smothered.

Shoving at the surface above, it won't budge. I catch a sliver in my thumb with a sting that feels way too real.

A coffin. Made of wood.

Pounding my fists against the sides makes only a deadened thud. As if there's earth packed against the outside.

Get me out! I'm not dead!

My screams die, muted, in my throat.

I claw at my mouth, straining the stitches, feeling skin tearing. I taste blood trickling into my mouth.

Jane.

A voice. Right in my ear.

I'm not alone in this coffin. I breathe in the sickly sweet smell of flowers gone rotten.

Stay with me, Jane.

I sense something reaching for me. A cold caress freezes the side of my neck. I pull away, but there's no room.

Don't touch me!

Stay with me.

I pull away. No space to move. I try rolling over, turning my back to it.

As I turn, it feels like I'm falling. For a second. Then I crash hard.

My eyes fly open. It's dark, but I can make out some things.

There's my bed beside me, my desk in the corner. My room.

I lie on the floor, hyperventilating. My lungs feel starved for oxygen.

Must have fallen off the bed, rolling over to get away from that thing.

Crouching on my knees with the blankets pooled around me, I feel my lips with my fingers. No stitches. No blood. Nothing.

I crawl over to my desk and click on the lamp.

I've had that same wild nightmare a couple of times since I got nailed. But never so bad, so vivid. And before, I was always alone in the coffin. Now something else is locked in there with me.

I lean against the wall. Can't get back in bed—can't risk picking up where I left off.

I can blame Lexi for some of the details in these nightmares. She's obsessed with horror flicks, filling my head with this stuff. Like the way they sew the corpses' eyelids shut to keep them from springing open during the funeral.

A full-body shiver runs through me. I can't shake the freeze left from that touch.

The sickeningly sweet smell is still in my nose. What was that thing in the coffin? Bringing me dead flowers like a valentine.

Stay with me, it said. Down in the dark.

"Go away," I whisper to the empty room. "Leave me alone."

But how do you break up with a nightmare?

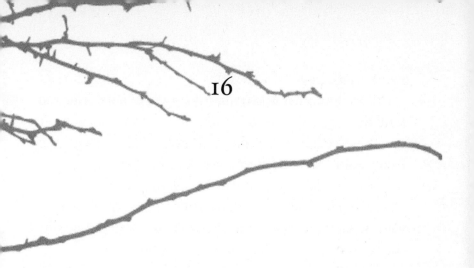

16

"Waking up in a coffin was bad enough. But now I'm trapped in there with that thing."

"A corpse with a crush on you," Lexi says. "Kinky."

We're sitting in Shipwrecks Cafe after school, talking nightmares. It's a little place on the waterfront that used to be a bar where the fishermen went after bringing in their day's catch. Now it's been converted into a haven for caffeine junkies, with some fishing decor to show its roots. Like the old photos of the local wrecks, boats that were victims of what they call "The Teeth," a string of spiky reefs that runs along this stretch of coast, and often takes bites out of boat hulls.

Lexi sips her coffee. "You know, that premature burial stuff isn't just urban legend. There are cases where coffins have been dug up and they've found scratch marks on the lids inside, broken fingernails stuck in the wood, bloody handprints."

I shudder, sipping my coffee to try to warm up. "And whatever it was, my undead date, its voice was so . . . strange."

"Strange how?"

"I don't know. It wasn't like a deep, dark voice. Sounded kind of . . . young, almost. I mean, not like a kid. But not grown-up either. Scary and kind of . . . sad." I shake my head. "All I know is I never want to hear it again."

"You need a restraining order for your dreams."

Sitting here by the windows, we've got a rain-blurred view down the street to the stormy waves crashing against the seawall, throwing up showers of white foam.

"Hey, Lexi. Is that your mom?"

Across the street, her mother's hard to miss in her fire-engine-red raincoat, her short spiky hair dyed platinum blond. She's sharing an umbrella with a skinny guy in a leather trench coat, his hair buzzed down to black stubble.

"Who's the guy?" I ask.

Lexi lets out a disgusted grunt. "He works at that tattoo place, Edge Ink. She met him when she went in to have hers changed."

"Never knew she had a tattoo. Where is it?"

"On her chest. She got it on her honeymoon. It's a heart broken in half, with a jagged edge. My father has the other half on his chest, with the matching edge so the two pieces fit together. Or he still had it years ago, last time I saw him."

"Did your mom get hers erased?"

"No. It's easier to just add on. So where the missing half is she got new orange flames inked in. Like the heart's on fire. She says it means she's red hot. And that my dad can go burn in hell."

We watch as they turn the corner, huddled together under their umbrella.

"The guy's name is Razor," she tells me. "He had it changed legally."

"How old is he?"

"Twenty-two." Lexi shudders. "Change the subject, quick. Let's stop talking about my nightmare and get back to yours."

I look down at the counter where I'm resting my elbows. It's actually a wooden railing salvaged from a shipwreck. There are hundreds of initials carved into the old wood, some enclosed in hearts, with equations like J.C. + B.R. = 4 EVER. Lexi calls it the love log.

"After your near-death experience, having coffin dreams is pretty understandable. Bringing a date along for the ride is an interesting twist."

We sip our coffee and watch the rain.

I always tell Lexi my dreams, nightmares and other delusions. She's great at analyzing them.

She was the one who found the pattern behind my shadow attacks. I'd always thought they just came out of nowhere, for no reason. But Lexi had the idea that there might be something bringing them on. Why did they happen when they did? Why so much time in between? What provoked them?

"Were you sick those times?" she asked me. "Upset about something? Depressed? Fighting with your parents? Think back. What else was going on? What led up to when your shadow turned against you?"

Those memories were still hyperreal, like if I shut

my eyes I'd be right there again. Made me feel panicky revisiting them, until I forced myself to shift the focus to what had happened just before.

I went over the hours and days leading up to the attacks. Different places, different seasons, different moods. Nothing in common that I could see.

I missed the link. But Lexi didn't.

It was right there in front of me. Just like the log I'm leaning on now, with all these equations adding one person to another. So many hearts and initials carved here.

But never mine. No love math for me. Because that was the link. The hidden pattern.

See, it all started with a valentine. My first crush, in second grade, was Scotty McNab. He sat behind me in class and was always getting me in trouble by making me laugh at the dumb jokes he whispered in my ear. He was a huge Hulk fan—every Halloween he went green—so the day before Valentine's I decided to make him a card. It was going to have a cutout of a roaring Hulk with a word bubble saying "Be Jane's valentine or I'll beat the crap out of you!" I was working on it at the kitchen table when I went looking in the cupboards for some glue.

But I found the drain cleaner instead, and my shadow forced me to drink it. I never sent that card. I turned scared and silent after that, forgot how to laugh at dumb jokes. And my crush got crushed.

My first date was a movie. Pretty tame, since we were only eleven, and there was a group of us. But me and Charlie Watts sat together and shared popcorn. Held hands in the dark where nobody could see. He made my heart flop around like a fish caught in my chest. I couldn't stop thinking about him after, and I was going to ask him over to play video games.

But the next day I found that fallen power line, and my shadow forced me to touch it.

Skip ahead to me at thirteen. Getting all hot and heavy with Jake Turner under the bleachers at the start of summer vacation. It was strictly over-the-clothes frisking and fumbling, but enough to get me in a fever.

Later that afternoon, while I was still flushed from Jake's hands, my shadow froze me up on the train tracks.

Lexi connected all these dots for me, linking my few romantic highlights with the attacks afterward.

"So what are you saying?" I asked. "Every time I really like a guy my shadow sabotages it and tries to kill me?"

"I'm just going by the evidence."

"But that's . . ."

"Nuts?"

"Yeah," I said.

"So tell me then—have you ever gone on a date, held hands, got felt up or whatever and your shadow didn't attack you?"

I tried to think, wanting to prove her wrong. Searching for any kind of romantic moment that hadn't ended badly for me. I came up blank.

"But what does it mean?" I finally asked.

"Maybe you've got a jealous shadow. It doesn't want

to share you with anybody. Wants to keep you for itself. And if you cheat on it—watch out. Sounds crazy, but it explains a lot."

Even after she pointed out the link, I wasn't convinced. The idea of me having a possessive shadow was plain insane.

The evidence was there, but was it really a pattern, or just paranoia? Or even coincidence?

I was never sure. Not until this last time, when my heart stopped and I flatlined.

Dying made a believer out of me.

17

The day I died the sun was shining and the sky was blue as a dream. After a week of wild storms that threatened to drown the town, with winds stripping the shingles off our roof, there wasn't a cloud to be seen all the way to the horizon.

It was a lazy Sunday October afternoon, and I dragged a lawn chair out so I could catch some of those rare autumn rays in the backyard. It was just warm enough for me to get away with wearing my bikini.

Dad was up on the roof trying to repair the damage before the next storm blew in. The quiet was broken by the *bang bang bang* of him nailing in new shingles.

I was deep into reading a thick and juicy romance novel of tropical lust shipwrecked on a deserted island. But my mind kept drifting away.

So I just lay there with my eyes closed, soaking up the sun, reliving a little forbidden thrill I'd had the day before, when I was over at the Blushing Rose.

* * *

I was watching the shop by myself while Mom dropped off some funeral wreaths.

The sound system was driving me nuts. Mom always plays this soft classical crap. She says it makes a soothing and nurturing atmosphere for the plants. It was soothing me into a coma. So I switched to the radio and found the throbbing beat of dance-club music.

With that cranked up loud, I got to work spritzing the plants around the shop. The air shuddered with the deep bass, vibrating my eardrums and the thousands of leaves, fronds and flowers around me. Felt like being inside some giant green beating heart.

Dancing and misting my way down the aisles, I was spraying the ferns when I caught something out of the corner of my eye. I wasn't alone.

I froze midspritz.

There he stood. Ryan. My secret sex god. Smiling at me.

Deafened by the music, I gave him a little wave. He waved back. Then I ran behind the counter and cut the noise.

"Sorry," I said into the sudden quiet. "Been kind of a slow day."

"Don't stop the party for me."

I could feel a blush heating my cheeks. "I've probably traumatized the tulips now. Shocked the lilies."

"Plants like a little rhythm. Gets the sap pumping."

I had to break away from his blue-green eyes. So I focused on the computer like I was checking something.

"So what can I do for you?"

Or do to you? Or can I just do you?

"Delivery," he said. "The truck's out back. I was beating on the door, but you had your own beat going on in here."

"Right, delivery. Come on in back. I'll open up for you."

I'll open up for you? I turned away quickly so he couldn't see my new blush.

He got busy unloading the shipment and I distracted myself making room in the cooler for the new order. Ryan had me sign off on the invoice.

"How did you get that?" he asked, pointing at the scratch across the back of my hand.

"Got in a fight with a cactus today."

"Hold on. I'll be right back."

I watched from the door as he disappeared into the back of the truck. When he jumped down, he was holding a potted plant with long, thick pointy leaves. "For you. Aloe vera."

"Why?"

Setting the pot down on a table, Ryan broke off one of the leaves where it was thickest. "Let's try this. Give me your hand." When I gave him a doubtful glance instead, he smiled. "Trust me."

I held out my wounded hand, and he took it. He squeezed the leaf with his free hand till it bled a few drops of clear liquid that dripped slow as honey onto my cut. Then he dropped the leaf and used his thumb to gently smooth the gel into my scratch.

"Old-school healing," Ryan told me. "Thousands of years old."

"You a witch doctor now?" I teased, trying to cover my full-body blush and racing heart.

Up close I could smell the green on him, a dizzying mix of all the plants, herbs and flowers he handled.

"In some parts of Asia they call aloe the crocodile's tongue, for the shape of its leaves."

"Really?" Could he feel my speeding pulse with his palm against mine?

"You wouldn't want a crocodile licking you, though. Their mouths are infested with parasites and bacteria. And their saliva . . ." He trailed off. "I'm kind of killing the mood, aren't I?"

We shared a nervous laugh. I could've listened to him talk about reptile spit all day.

"Keep going," I said, meaning the aloe rubdown. Meaning whatever.

"Well, if their bite doesn't kill you, all those nasty critters in their saliva will. It's because of the croc's bad dental hygiene, which makes their mouths breeding grounds for all kinds of germs and diseases—" He broke off and let me have my hand back. "I'm going to shut up before I make you nauseous. Anyway, I gotta go. More deliveries down the coast."

I followed him to the back door. "Am I healed?"

"Your witch doctor prescribes a few drops twice a day."

As he was getting in the truck I called, "Thanks for the tongue."

He gave me a wave. "Any time."

* * *

"He said that? Any time?" Lexi asked, when I replayed the whole thing to her over the phone that night.

"Yeah. What do you think he meant?"

"He meant any time, anywhere, anything."

That was what I was hoping, what I was scared of.

"I wish, but I can't. You know what'll happen to me if I get hot and heavy with him."

"Yeah, I know. You're scared it might set off your psycho shadow. But look, you flirted, you touched, he gave you a rubdown—and nothing bad happened, right?"

"But if I try anything, what if it brings on another attack? You were there last time, with the train. You saw."

"That was like four years ago. And I really don't know what I saw. Maybe it was some weird hallucination we shared. Who knows? But it's been a long time, and that thing never came back. Whatever it was. The whole jealous-shadow theory was my stupid idea."

"Maybe."

"You've been a total nun. You can't live in fear forever. Go for it."

Lexi's advice, Ryan's touch and my own feelings came together as I was lying in the sun in the backyard that October day. I knew what I had to do.

The afternoon had gone quiet. Dad was taking a break from nailing shingles up on the roof and had gone inside for lunch. It was just me, the sun and the clear blue sky.

Should I call or text Ryan? I had his number and contact info from the shop. Texting seemed safer. If I called him I might say something dumb I couldn't take back. Say too much, or say it wrong.

The night before, Lexi had told me I should just show up at the greenhouse. It would be like our Garden of Eden. I would play Eve to his Adam. She'd said to just grab Ryan, throw him down in the flowers and feed him one of those hothouse apples. Or in my case—Lexi said, playing the snake—give him my cherry.

Sending him a text was less risky, and less raunchy.

So I got up and headed inside for my phone. I felt kind of dizzy, maybe from too much sun or just from standing up too fast. But by the time I reached the steps to the back porch, I had to stop and steady myself. Waiting a moment for the feeling to fade only made it worse.

Then my legs started to shake.

Trying to focus, I noticed the tools Dad had left out on the porch. There was the nail gun he was using for the shingles, loaded with one-inch nails. It looked big and bulky, like some kind of alien weapon.

Everything was going fuzzy around the edges, my mind hazing over, but I couldn't stop staring at it.

I wasn't going to touch the gun. But my shadow had other ideas. With the sun at my back it was sprawled across the steps.

As the shadow of my arm stretched out, it pulled my left hand along with it, that darkness reaching to wrap around the handle. I fought against it.

My hand shook in the air above the gun, and I almost thought I could beat the thing. It was a tug-of-war. But an electric whine filled the air, tunneling through my ears into my head till I couldn't struggle anymore, and I could only watch as my left hand joined its shadow on the handle, lifting the gun to my head.

The cool muzzle pressed against my skull, just behind my ear. My finger found the trigger. There was a loud pop when it fired. Then a sharp sting.

I dropped the gun. It banged off the stairs and landed on the ground at my feet.

The numbing fog that held me made everything seem very far away. Even the pain was just a mosquito bite. Staring down at the gun, I saw something dripping on it.

Red paint? I thought in a daze. Where's that coming from?

I noticed more paint running down my left arm and side, felt its warm wetness. I started to look up, like it might be raining red from the sky. As I stretched my head back, the mosquito bite flared into a white-hot needle in my skull.

Falling to my knees, I stared at the ground, the dirt soaking up the blood spurting from me. I knew if I looked over *it* would be there. My shadow. Standing near me. Waiting.

Then I felt myself being lifted up. My shadow was taking me away now. I was done. My eyes were closing forever.

But before they shut I saw a face above me. Mom. I was in her arms.

"Stay with me!" she was shouting. "Hold on!"

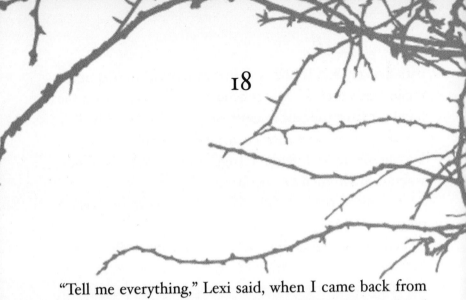

18

"Tell me everything," Lexi said, when I came back from the dead. "What did you see? The light? Spirits? Dead relatives? Dead pets?"

I told her what I'd seen. But only her. Mom and Dad were worried about me enough already without more evidence that their daughter was deeply disturbed.

Good thing my shadow's aim was bad. The nail just missed an artery or I would have bled out before I got to the hospital. Even then it was almost too late to save me. My heart stopped after it ran out of blood to pump.

I blacked out before Mom got me into the car. After that I remember nothing until suddenly, like coming wide awake from a dreamless sleep, I found myself floating above a bed in the emergency room. Below, the doctors were working frantically on me.

But I had a ghost's body now. Lighter than air, with hands I could see through.

Mom was close by, leaning on Dad like he was the only thing keeping her from collapsing. Her shirt was soaked with my blood. Dad's mouth hung open as if he was fighting for each breath, trying to breathe for me.

I wanted to tell them sorry. And say goodbye. I had no voice, but I was still trying to speak, when—

There was an explosion of light above me. I looked up and found a blazing brightness.

It shined through me—like it was taking an X-ray of my soul. Burning away all my panic and pain.

So beautiful and intense, it made me feel like I'd been blind since birth and was seeing for the first time.

I felt its pull and started drifting upward. This was it. I was going away, forever.

Taking one last glance at that empty body, I looked at the doctors and nurses struggling to bring me back. At Dad, so shocked and pale he seemed like a ghost himself.

And that was when I saw *it*! Standing next to him was my shadow.

I recognized it. The thing that had haunted me since I was little. My childhood assassin. Here to watch me die, with hungry, wet black eyes. It was three-dimensional now, dark and shiny, like a body dipped in paint.

Its stare was locked on me. Not me in the bed, but up where I was now, rising toward the light.

I looked away from it and gazed up into the whiteness. I was leaving my shadow behind with everything else. There was no darkness where I was going.

Reaching up, my phantom arm passed deep into the glow, melting into it. Sending a thrill of warmth down through me, soothing away my sadness. I lifted my face to taste that perfect sunshine. So close.

But then everything went wrong.

I was grabbed from below. Even in this body made of nothing but air, I felt something pulling me back.

I looked down into the dark eyes of my shadow. It had one arm raised to catch me. I kicked out to free myself as it held tight, dragging me away from the light.

A shock of cold ran up my leg.

This thing ate the light. It was sucking me in too. I couldn't break away. It was like a hole cut out of the air, a mouth of darkness.

And it swallowed me up.

I found myself surrounded by blackest night, cold nothingness. I've never felt so hopeless and despairing.

But I wasn't alone. I could sense something near me, hidden in the dark.

When I was little I once asked Mom if my shadow had a life of its own. Now I knew it did.

Later I told Lexi it was like that thing they do on *Star Trek*—a mind meld. Where you share someone else's thoughts.

Because just when I thought this night might last forever, something reached out and grabbed hold of me. That cold touch ignited a flash of light.

And then it was like having a slide show projected inside my mind. I saw a series of pictures go by.

But somehow I knew they were more than just pictures.

Memories. Of faces I'd never seen, places I'd never been. Pieces of a stranger's life melding into me.

First, there was a view of a rocky coastline not so different from Edgewood's, a harbor with a small blink-and-you'll-miss-it town. I spotted a little blue house. There was a woman standing in the front yard, looking off down the road as if waiting for someone to come home.

Who was she? Sadness flooded through me. The ache of loss and loneliness. Somehow I knew what her laugh would sound like, and her voice too.

It was surreal, feeling all this for someone I'd never met.

Then, I saw inside the blue house. And upstairs, a room that wasn't mine, but where everything was so familiar. Everything from the star map on the ceiling that would glow when the light was turned off to the terrarium with a little frog sitting in a pool of water. From the poster on the wall of a model in a bikini lying on some tropical beach to the small basketball hoop hung on the closet door to the view out the window of the woods behind the house.

The image changed to show a pond in those woods, with swampy water bright green with algae. A jar full of freshly collected tadpoles held up to the sunlight. A sense of discovery and happiness.

But then it was like a storm cloud blocked out the sun. Everything changed. At the edge of the pond, under the cover of the trees, stood a tall man, his face hidden in shade. I could feel his eyes watching.

Fear shot through me, and an urge to run.

But the next flash showed him up close. And it was too late to escape. I could see him clearly now. He was bald and skeletally thin. His face was all sharp edges, like it had been carved with a hatchet. A beak of a nose, hollowed cheeks and a brow that jutted out above cold dark eyes.

A big black bird rode on his shoulder. A crow. They had the same eyes, deep and lifeless.

Panic spiked through me. I didn't want to see any more. Wanted to get away. Escape!

The skeleton man was grinning, reaching out a bony hand. I knew his touch would mean something worse than death. But I was trapped. That hand grabbed hold, digging in with fingers like ice. I was lost, a prisoner to the memory. And I knew the real nightmare was just beginning. I begged for a voice so I could scream.

But then—

A world away, the doctors shocked my heart back to life.

The nightmare vision cut to black.

I felt the shadow trying to hold on and keep me in that midnight place. But I was torn from its grasp. Its scream ripped through the dark as I pulled free.

That scream followed me as I fell through an infinity of blackness. Returning to my body and my beating heart.

I hope it's over now.

Whatever that thing was, I hope I finally lost it. Left it behind in the dark when I broke away.

Maybe I'm just fooling myself, but it keeps me sane to think that.

When I had to explain how I "accidentally" shot myself with the nail gun, I just told them I'd picked the thing up because I was curious. The gun was heavy and slipped in my hand. I must have hit the trigger somehow.

I'm not saying they totally bought it, not with my history. But there was a strange detail that supported my lie. The nail was fired through the left side of my skull. And as every good cop knows, when somebody tries to commit suicide by shooting themselves in the head, they always use their dominant hand to hold the gun. I'm right-handed, so I would have shot through the right side of my head. This made my lie believable enough. I'm not a lefty, but I guess my shadow was.

I hope it's gone for good. Now it only haunts me in my nightmares.

It could still be waiting for me on the other side. I'll worry about that when I'm old and gray. As long as it stays there.

Some things belong in the dark.

19

"Welcome to my dream," says the girl on the screen.

I'm in computer class, where we're working on graphics and Web design. Our big project for the term is to build our own Web pages about whatever we want. Right now we're taking sneak peeks at each other's works in progress.

Valerie is running us through her site on the big screen at the front. She calls it My Decadent Dream Closet. It opens with her welcoming us in, reaching for a door with golden light shining out around the edges. The buildup makes you think there's magic on the other side, like it's the wardrobe to Narnia or something.

Instead, the site is a tour of her huge walk-in closet, cataloging a massive collection of clothes, shoes and accessories. It's a fashion fantasy museum that lets you click on items for detailed descriptions. As an extra feature you can build your own ensemble, putting together an outfit from her collection.

"I'm still working on that," Valerie says. "I want to make it so you get graded on how good your taste is."

"She makes me gag," Lexi mumbles beside me.

I elbow her quiet.

Miss Jankowski says, "Well organized. A popular concept for our cultural craze of consumerism."

After that we get a couple of gaming fan sites with lots of blood and gore. If only some of these mutant zombie aliens would invade Valerie's closet for a bloody battle. She could add a feature where you build your own ensemble from the scattered body parts.

Then comes the moment I've been dreading. It's Max's turn. I think he took this class just to torture Lexi. His Max to the Max site is devoted to himself, of course, and his crap band. Basically it's a photo gallery of moody shots of him with the other members in the background, a brief bio that makes him sound badass, and then there's the video Lexi shot for him, along with extra footage of him competing in a Battle of the Bands in the city last year.

"It's got some style," Miss J says. "But the layout is a bit simple. Kind of a basic cookie-cutter site."

"But who cares what the frame looks like when the painting's a masterpiece, right?" Max grins.

"Well, when you get back from your ego trip, you should fix those dead links. And if you want to include a blog, it should be more than a list of celebrities you want to 'bang.'"

"My turn to gag," I tell Lexi, who's nervously chipping the polish off her nails.

"Next we have Jane and Lexi. You've partnered up for your site? What's the subject?"

"It's for my mother's store. A flower shop."

"Let's take a look." Miss J clicks it up on the big screen.

Our Blushing Rose site opens with a video Lexi dreamed up. It's like one of those perfume ads where you can't tell what they're selling till the end. It starts in black-and-white with Lexi on the beach in a long dark dress, looking sadly out at the gray waves under a gray sky. She glances down and sees a rose petal in the sand, glowing bright crimson, the only color in this monotone world. There's a trail of petals leading up the beach. She follows them, like they're bread crumbs in a fairy tale, onto the seawall and then into town. Rushing along the deserted streets, she tracks the petals on the pavement until they end. Then as she looks up from the ground we see where they came from. The Blushing Rose stands out from everything else in a burst of brilliant color. The image freezes on the storefront.

Then the home page for the shop comes up with contact and ordering info.

"Nice," Miss J says. "You might want to shorten the ad up front. You can lose customers with long intros. Or you could run it as a banner ad on top so there's no delay entering the site."

I did most of the layout, as well as the camerawork, following Lexi through town in the early morning so we had the streets to ourselves. She did a lot of the graphics. My favorite part is the blushing effect I did on the two roses that bookend the shop's name at the top. I took a pure white rose and made it blush deep red, running the change on a loop.

"You all have to start focusing on making these sites

functional. Design is the fun part. Now you have to make them work. Looks will only get you so far." Miss J aims that last bit at Max.

She makes the rounds of the class, fixing our glitches.

"I'm thinking of doing a sequel," Lexi says. "The shop needs a whole campaign, to keep people coming back to see what's next."

"But none of your experimental stuff. My mom isn't into the weirdness."

Mom already vetoed a couple of Lexi's edgier pieces. One had a rose bursting into flame, like a long-stemmed torch. The other showed the life cycle of a rose, sped up so it went from bud to full bloom to wilting in ten seconds, with the message *Life is short. Stop and smell the roses.* Mom said, "Too depressing. People don't buy dead flowers, or flammable ones."

"How about some kind of fairy-tale rip-off?" Lexi says.

I yawn for the hundredth time today.

"You listening, Jane?"

"Yeah, I'm just so wiped out."

"I've got an idea. Why don't we do Sleeping Beauty? You could star this time."

I laugh. Sometimes it does feel like I'm stuck in my own dark fairy tale. But nothing the Brothers Grimm ever dreamed up. This one comes from the Creep Sisters.

Call it *Sleepless Jane.*

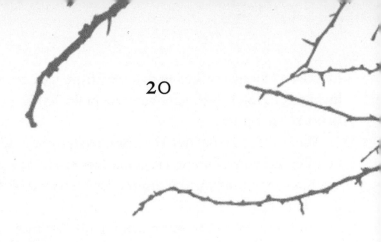

20

The rain's coming down with a vengeance, drumming on the roof of the car and streaming off the windshield so it feels like we're underwater, in a submarine.

Dad's bringing me home from my weekly checkup.

"Dr. Simon says you're a medical marvel. No problems. No impairment. No danger signs."

My neurologist just took my brain out for a test drive, examining my sensory perception, memory and motor skills.

"I even passed the drunk test," I say.

"What's that?"

"You know, the same thing you give drivers when you pull them over to see if they've been drinking. Close your eyes and touch the tip of your nose with your index finger. Stand on one foot. Walk a straight line. Except Doc Simon didn't give me a Breathalyzer."

"But can you do this?" Dad sticks out his tongue and touches the tip of his nose with it.

I shake my head. "I did not inherit that amazing genetic ability."

"Good thing you got your genes from our mother," he says, turning to make his snarling bulldog face to me. "This is not a pretty picture."

I snarl back. He texted Mom before we left the hospital to let her know how my checkup went. She'll be closing up at the shop right about now. It's getting dark out.

The steady rumble of the rain and the even beat of the wipers back and forth are making me drowsy. I yawn hugely.

"Rest up, Boo. We'll be home soon."

Turning off the coast highway, we pass over the ridge and head down into Edgewood. The trees tower above us on the hillsides. The flooded road looks like a flowing black river.

I lean back in the seat. So tired. Closing my eyes, I start to drift off.

But when I open them again, only a moment later, something feels wrong. It's suddenly freezing in here. We're still driving in the tunnel of trees, with the evergreens looming over us, but now it seems dark as midnight out there. A shudder runs through me, ice water in my veins.

I turn to ask Dad to put the heater on. And my heart seizes up.

He's not there! My shadow is. Sitting behind the wheel. A faceless black body, gleaming wet.

No! I'm not seeing this. That's not real. I'm still asleep. Dreaming.

It looks over at me, with eyes like bubbles of liquid tar.

Wake up! Wake up *now.*

The shadow raises its arm.

I try to scream, but the sound gets strangled in my throat. If the shadow touches me I'll die. I know it.

I jump when my arm lifts up on its own, matching that thing's movement, following its lead. The shadow leans forward to press a dark hand against the windshield. Helpless, I do the same a second after, my palm flattened on the cold glass.

But that black hand doesn't stop there. It passes through the windshield, out into the night. Where I can't follow. Still, I feel as if it's dragging part of me along.

I watch that arm reaching ahead, like an inky tentacle in the shine of the headlights. Farther and farther. Taking me with it. My body stays stiff in the seat, but I feel like I'm being stretched—not my skin and bone, somewhere even deeper. Making me tremble.

Gotta wake up! I'm in the car with Dad. Safe.

I can sense that shadow arm, like some kind of phantom limb—the wind and rain passing through it. Extending as if it's elastic.

But I'm not. I'm being pulled inside out. Like that time on the train tracks when I felt a snap and my shadow separated from me. It's stretching me too far.

The tentacle reaches into the trees now.

Can't take it. Breaking apart. I'm shaking wildly.

"Hang on!"

Dad's voice breaks me out of it. Jerking me awake.

My head whips around to see him there behind the wheel.

I'm still shaking all over. But it's not just me. The whole car is shuddering.

What is this?

"Dad?"

He stomps on the brakes. Everything's a blur through the windshield. We're swerving. He's fighting with the wheel as the rear end fishtails. I brace myself on the dashboard.

The car skids to a bumpy stop. Breathless, I look over at Dad. Everything keeps shaking for a minute. Like an earthquake.

"Jane. You okay?"

I nod. "What's going on? What was that?"

He points ahead, and in the headlights I see a mountain of mud, broken branches and fallen trees.

"Landslide. Barely missed driving right into it."

I stare dazed at the chaos outside. What just happened? Am I still dreaming?

"Is it—is it over?" I ask, not sure if I'm talking about the dream or the slide.

"Seems like it. But both lanes are blocked." Dad unbuckles his seat belt. "Wait in the car."

"Why? Where are you going?"

"I have to set out road flares before someone else crashes into this mess."

He's always a cop. Never off duty.

Pulling up the hood of his slicker, he heads out into the downpour. I watch him pop the trunk and grab the flares. He jogs down the road and ignites them. Bright yellow fireworks lighting up the night.

Trembling, I hug myself against the cold.

Don't lose it, Jane. It was just a nightmare. All over now.

But that's no dream blocking the road.

When Dad passes by the car again he's on his walkie-talkie, calling in to the station. He holds up his hand, telling me to stay put. I watch him in the glare of the headlights as he inspects the landslide.

After a couple of minutes, I'm feeling claustrophobic in here, like I've breathed all the air in the car and I'm starting to smother. Gotta get out!

So I grab my slicker from the backseat, pull it on and step into the gusting rain.

I notice two cars stopping near the flares back down the road.

The freezing wind helps clear my head. Deep breaths.

Dad's checking out the damage with his flashlight. Half the hillside has fallen down, burying the road. Splintered branches, massive tree trunks, muck and boulders.

I walk around the edges. The drivers from the other cars have come up for a peek at the mess too. One guy has even got his cell phone out, taking pictures of it.

Dad steps through the debris, aiming his flashlight at something, bending down for a closer look. He said to wait here, but I find myself wandering over to see what he's looking at.

He's on his talkie. "I'm going to need more backup on this. I've got a ten-ninety-five out here."

I try to remember what that's police code for.

"Repeat last transmission," says the voice on the other end.

I'm right behind him, close enough to glance over his

shoulder. Following the beam of his flashlight, I see what he's focused on.

I gasp, flinching.

"You heard me right. We've got a ten-ninety-five. Human remains."

There's a skull caught in the light.

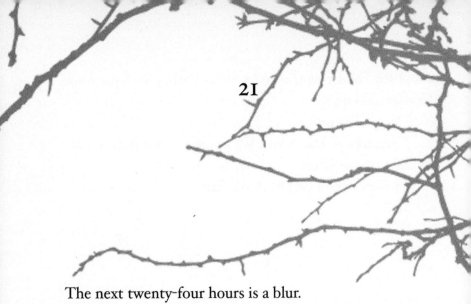

21

The next twenty-four hours is a blur.

After the landslide and seeing that skull, I guess I was in shock, because my memory is patchy. I remember Mom coming to pick me up, and hugging me so tight I could barely breathe. She drove me home, while Dad stayed behind to secure the site of the remains.

I think me and Mom talked for a while in the kitchen, but I can't recall any of it. I was running on autopilot, nodding when I was supposed to and mumbling one-word answers. Then I took a long hot shower to thaw out. Weak as a baby, I collapsed in bed wearing my bathrobe. I was dead to the world, and thankfully dreamless, till morning.

Dad came home around breakfast to change into his uniform and grab something to eat before heading out again. He gave us an update between bites.

They called in backup from the city, which sent a forensics team to process the scene. A road crew was waiting for them to finish, to clear the debris away. Dad said it's not uncommon to come across old bones in the forest along the coast. The Indians were here for a thousand years before us, laying their dead to rest in the woods.

"Gave us a scare, didn't it, Boo? How you holding up?"

"I'm okay," I told him.

Then he was gone again, with a thermos of coffee and a kiss from Mom.

Of course, I was far from okay. Mom said I should stay home from school, but I wanted to get out, needed the distraction. And just *had* to see Lexi so I could tell her everything.

But giving her the full story had to wait till we were alone, so she got the highlights as I stumbled through my classes.

It's only *now,* sitting with Lexi in Shipwrecks Cafe, that the shock wears off. I replay everything for her, from the nightmare to the slide to the skull. By the end my head feels clear, and the world comes back into focus.

"You're turning into a real spooky chick," she tells me.

"Always was one."

We're tucked away in a cozy back corner away from the crowd, drinking hot chocolate.

"And now you're famous," she says, looking at the newspaper on the table.

I shake my head in dismay. The story made page two of the national paper. I'm amazed they got it out so fast, almost as quick as the online news sites Lexi showed me earlier.

The headline says *Constable Makes Grisly Discovery.* But

it's the photo that gives me the chills. It must have been taken by that driver with the cell phone who came up to view the landslide.

The picture freezes that terrible moment when I saw what Dad had spotted in the tangled mass of branches and mud. We're caught in the headlights of our own parked car. Dad's leaning forward, shining his flashlight on the skull, making it glow white against the black earth. And I'm behind him, the hood of my slicker blown back by the wind, face as pale as bone. My naturally wide-eyed, startled look is taken to the extreme. It's like my eyes are bugging out, with my mouth hanging open in a gasp.

I push the paper way, not wanting to see the image anymore.

"So what do you think about all this insanity?" I ask.

"Don't totally freak out. We get landslides and mudslides every rainy season around here."

"I mean about my nightmare right before the slide. What about that?"

Lexi sips her hot chocolate. "You've been having nonstop nightmares since you came back from the dead. Every time you take a nap you're getting locked in a coffin or chased by your shadow. Sure, if I were you I'd be paranoid too. I just don't know if you can blame a dream for a natural disaster."

"Maybe. But what about the skull? That was real. No dream."

"Yeah. But like your dad said, they've discovered

Indian burial grounds around Edgewood before. Remember when they were building the new mall and had to delay construction after digging up those old native bones?"

"So you don't think my shadow had anything to do with making the slide happen?"

"How is that possible?"

"How is any of this—my whole history—possible?"

I start to hyperventilate, and Lexi reaches over to squeeze my hand.

"Breathe, Jane. Just breathe."

It takes me a minute to get a grip and slow my heart down.

"And besides," she says. "You ditched that shadow thing back in the Great Beyond, right?"

I nod. I have to believe that. Need it to be true.

"Why me?" It's the question I've been asking since I was little.

Lexi shrugs. "Who knows? You're like a paranormal perfect storm. A magnet for bad luck."

"Thanks. They can add that to my school yearbook profile." I glance over at the newspaper. In the picture's caption I'm identified as "the constable's daughter." "How's this for a headline—*Psycho Jane Strikes Again?*"

Lexi checks out the photo.

"That's a great shot of you, really cinematic." She sees everything with a moviemaker's eye. "You could be the next great horror movie scream queen."

I shake my head. "I get enough scares just being me."

"I hate to say it. But by tomorrow, this whole thing is going to go viral."

I groan, burying my head in my hands. "They should just use that for my yearbook photo. It's how everybody's going to remember me anyway. The spookiest chick in town."

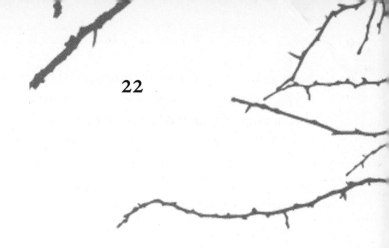

22

I gaze out the window, watching the world drown. Rain. Rain. Rain.

Two days after the landslide, I'm back at the Blushing Rose. Mom's out making deliveries. That used to be my job after school and on weekends, but my brain injury means I'm not allowed to drive right now.

Mom thought I might want to stay home from work and school, after the trauma of the slide and seeing those remains, and all that's gone wrong lately. But I need this everyday normalness. Gotta keep busy.

School today was surreal. With that photo of me and the skull showing up everywhere, I thought the smart-ass remarks and general harassment were going to get worse. But no, everybody's avoiding me, as if I've got some kind of infectious supernatural virus. Good thing I've got my Creep Sister to keep me company.

I take a seat behind the counter. Outside, the world is all shades of gray. But in here it's an explosion of color.

There's a lot of family history in this shop. Mom inherited it from her mother. Both of us spent our childhoods helping out here, doing homework in the back, where it's like a pocket-sized jungle crowded with plants. And this is where Mom and Dad first met.

He says it was a beauty-and-the-beast kind of thing.

They went to the same schools growing up. But they were on completely different planets. She was the smart shy girl, pretty but not in a showy way. He was the hell-raising son of the old head constable, the town's top cop. Dad was on the football, rugby, wrestling and boxing teams. Anywhere you got to lay down some hits and get hit. He says it was his way of fighting back against living under the constable's laws at home and everywhere else. In one of his school yearbooks he was named most likely to go out in a blaze of glory. He was living in fast-forward, like there was no tomorrow.

But that all ended when the constable had a heart attack writing a speeding ticket and died out on the highway.

Leaving behind a huge black hole in Dad, with nothing left to fight.

When Dad showed up at the Blushing Rose to pick up the wreaths for the funeral, Mom was watching the shop, like I am now.

She says he gave her a scare when she looked up and saw him standing there. He was wearing a suit, but his face was all bruised, with a split lip and a fresh black eye. Looking like he had just stumbled in off a battlefield, he had that shell-shocked stare. Didn't say a word, but she knew who he was and brought out the wreaths.

"Sorry about your father," she said.

"What do I do now?" he asked.

Mom wasn't sure what he meant, so she told him it was already paid for by the town council.

"What do I do?" he kept saying.

She could only shake her head. He was the most lost thing she'd ever seen.

He gave her another scare when he started crying, leaning on the counter. Mom never saw anyone cry so hard without making a sound. And this wasn't just any-body, but the legendary local thug. The Bulldog. So now she was asking herself, What do I do?

And what she did was a small brave gesture. Mom reached over and patted his hand, with its swollen knuck-les and scabbed fingers. Like petting a strange dog when you don't know if it's going to lick your hand or bite it. Her touch was just a little thing, but it changed every-thing.

When he finally ran out of tears, Dad caught his reflection in the glass doors of the coolers. Eyes puffy and bloodshot. "I can't let them see me like this."

"It's your father's funeral. They'll understand."

"No. Can't let them see me."

So Mom ended up lending him her sunglasses.

He tried them on. It was hard getting the glasses to sit right and keep from slipping down the busted bridge of his nose. "Can you still tell? How do I look?"

Mom told him what he wanted to hear.

"Like the Terminator."

And he laughed. A small miracle on a very bad day.

Beauty meets the beast.

I never get tired of hearing that story. Where they started out. Right here, in this spot.

I smile, and it turns into a yawn so massive and wide I hear my jaws pop.

Haven't had a customer in half an hour. The white noise of the rain tapping on the front window blends in with the hum of the refrigerators behind me keeping the flowers cool and fresh.

Since the shock of the landslide I'm getting maybe three hours of sleep a night. I keep jumping awake, from nightmares I can't remember.

I catch myself nodding off, my head bobbing up with a snort. I blink my eyes wide.

Maybe I should crank up some music, something loud to—

Thump!

I flinch at the sound behind me. Spinning around in the chair, I look for what made it. Maybe something fell over in one of the fridges. The glass doors are fogged from the humidity, so I get up and open them.

Cold air blows over me as I lean in. No vases toppled over, no mess.

I take a peek in the back room but can't spot anything wrong there either. The noise could have been coming from the back alley. Maybe they're picking up the garbage.

I head back to my chair.

Thump!

Louder. I face the fridges. Definitely seems to be coming from there. Maybe the motor on the cooler is acting up.

I step closer to the fogged doors.

Thump! Thump!

What is that? Can't be good.

THUMP!

I jump as something hits the glass. And I see—

No!

There's a hand pressed against the inside of the door. I back up into the counter. Can't be. But a palm is flattened on the glass. It pulls away, leaving a cleared patch in the condensation, and a smear of red. Blood?

It smacks the glass harder.

I gasp, stunned. I just looked in there. Nowhere to hide. No way. My eyes are lying to me.

But something wants out of there.

I move away as it starts pounding with both hands, leaving more bloody streaks. The glass is going to crack under the beating.

No! No way!

One more hit knocks the door open a few inches.

Chilled air drifts from the gap like a breath of mist. In the sudden silence, I stand shaking, staring at the smeared bloody palm prints.

The escaping mist carries a sound with it. A whisper.

Jane.

No. I'm not hearing that!

Jane.

I want to kick the door shut. To run. Get away, before whatever's connected to those hands steps out.

But I can't move. Can't even—

Oh, God! What's that? Something's moving.

Fingers, stained red, curl around the door's edge.

No. No. No!

I reach behind me blindly for anything to fight with. Scissors. Before I can grab them something touches my hand. I whip my head around. Ready to scream.

Mom's standing there.

"You okay?" she asks. "Didn't you hear me?"

I can't speak. I glance back at the fridge.

And see nothing. No fingers. No blood. No streaks in the condensation. The cooler door is shut tight.

"Jane?" Mom's giving me a worried frown.

I find my voice. "S-sorry. Sorry. I don't know what . . ."

"You look flushed. Any fever?"

She puts the back of her hand against my forehead.

"No, Mom."

"Any headache?"

"Nothing. Really. I just . . . I thought I heard something in the coolers. Something wrong."

Mom goes to open the door that was dripping with blood a moment ago.

Don't! I want to shout. Something's in there.

She pokes her head inside. I hold my breath, waiting for her scream. She checks the thermometer. Looking over her shoulder, I see only the flowers and arrangements. Nothing more.

"Seems fine." She closes the door.

I fake a normal face real quick. "Good. That's good. Um . . . if you don't need me, I'm gonna take off now."

She starts filing away her delivery slips. "You want to wait around an hour and I'll drive you home?"

"That's okay." I reach for my coat. "I could use some air."

"Well, call and let me know when you get home, then."

I nod, grabbing an umbrella on my way out.

The rain's coming down hard, turning the street into a shallow stream. Even with the umbrella I'm going to get soaked, but I don't care. I need to get away from here.

23

I'm too shaky and wired to go home, can't be alone right now. I need somebody to talk me down.

So I go see my Creep Sister.

Lexi reads my face as soon as she opens her door.

"That bad?"

I shiver a nod, and she lets me in out of the rain. Warming up over a mug of coffee in her room above the garage, I replay what just happened.

"Are you sure you weren't dreaming?" she says. "You said you were nodding off right before."

"I don't know. It felt so real, Lexi."

"Yeah. But the past few days . . . I mean, you're getting no sleep, that nail's screwing with your wiring, you just cheated death by landslide, and you're superstressed."

Now that I've put a little distance between me and what happened in the shop, my own doubts are starting to creep in.

"I feel like I'm losing it."

"You're safe now. Just breathe, Jane."

I let out a shaky sigh, trying to get my speeding heart

to slow down. The rain patters on the roof, soft and hushing.

"There's this thing I read about," Lexi says. "Sort of a sleep disorder. *Hypnagogia*."

"What's that?"

"It's like having waking dreams. When you're half-asleep, and the line between conscious and unconscious gets blurred. It can happen if you're stressed and sleep deprived, or it can be a side effect of some medications."

"I'm taking a fistful of meds every day."

"With all those drugs in your system, maybe you're having a bad reaction."

"Real bad." I drink the last of my coffee, letting it defrost me. "You think that's what it was? Felt like more than a dream."

"These hypnagogia things are supposed to seem hyper-real. Where you're still aware of your actual surroundings, but your subconscious splices a little something extra into the scene."

"So it's like a hallucination?"

"Yeah. But that doesn't make you a lunatic."

"This stuff ever happen to you?"

"No. I mean, I only get maybe three hours of sleep a night, but I don't feel deprived. I'm just wired." She bugs out her eyes at me.

I smile. Lexi's my real shrink and dream doctor.

I set my empty mug down on her desk. Caffeine probably wasn't a great idea. Feels like I'm going to jump out of my skin. I try to walk it off, pacing around her room.

Lexi's been working on a new project, and it covers the wall above her desk. Guess I'm the inspiration for it.

A gallery of images show what the Great Beyond looks like. Lots of glowing doorways, and heavenly cloudscapes with gates opened wide. The phantom souls of the newly dead hovering above their own lifeless bodies. Helpful spirits pointing out the way to the other side.

"So, Lexi, when you were digging all this up, did you find anything that was like my own bad trip?"

"You're kind of unique when it comes to these near-death things. Some of what you saw fits the usual story. You did the out-of-body stuff, saw the light and went for it. But then you took a wrong turn."

"Seriously wrong."

"Most people get *life reviews,* like a replay of their greatest hits. From their first breath to last."

"I got one of those, but it wasn't *my* life."

I've rerun that vision in my head a thousand times, trying to make sense of it. That little seaside town, the blue house. The woman waiting out front. There was such an overwhelming feeling of loss at the sight of her. Then, upstairs in the guy's room. That stuff seems easier to understand, memories of a lost life. But then the vision turned dark and strange, with the bald skeleton man. A crow on his shoulder. What does it all mean?

"Where did you find this stuff?" I lean in to study the afterlife images.

"I joined an online support group for the resurrected, pretending to be one of them. They call themselves *Second*

Chancers. I told them your story, saying it was mine. You know, to see if anybody had a similar experience."

Lexi loves these online encounters where she can be anybody. She uses about a dozen cyber aliases and personalities.

"Did you find any like mine?"

"Well, ninety-nine percent of these visions are positive. Even a few atheists found religion after what they saw. The resurrected come back renewed, and the only regret they have is that they didn't get to stay in the light. But they find peace knowing it's there waiting for them when their time finally comes."

I spot a welcoming spirit in one picture, in the shine from the other side. I remember how that light felt, sweeter than anything ever.

But there were no guiding spirits waiting to show me the way. And no peace now, knowing what else is waiting.

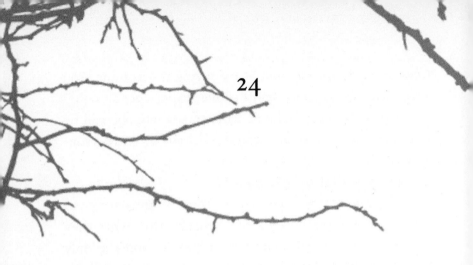

24

Sanctuary.

I find a quiet spot to sit near the back of St. Mary's, a cozy little church in the center of Edgewood. One of the oldest places around here, it was built using wood from the ancient forest they cut down to make room for the town. Behind the simple altar there's a stained-glass scene of Mary in mourning, sitting on a rock and looking out to a stormy sea.

But I'm not really here to claim sanctuary. I'm the floral director for the wedding that's just about to start.

Mom usually handles this stuff while I watch the shop. But I didn't want to be left alone there.

I breathe in the smell of incense, roses and burning candles, relaxing for the first time in days. I already set up the arrangements, handed out bouquets to the brides-maids, tied bundles of white lilies to the pews along the center aisle, decorated the altar with pink carnations and filled the flower girl's basket with crimson rose petals. Now I hang around for the show. Such a love junkie.

My addiction to romance novels started years back.

Maybe it comes from having a lusty heart, or maybe I crave what I can't have. I mean, it's never going to be me at the altar.

I tried making up my own stories, to live out my fantasies that way. I used to be good with words. Writing was my *thing*. Like Lexi and her movies, words were how I made sense of stuff.

But everything I wrote came out wrong. Where I was trying for romance, passion and desire, everything turned all doom and gloom. So I quit.

Now I just stick to the love library in my closet.

I can't take any chances. I have to keep my distance from Ryan, and every other guy. No flirting, no messages, nothing. I'm still playing by my shadow's rules. Because as long as I've stayed alone, it's let me live. I want to believe I got rid of that thing, but I'm not going to risk it.

The priest steps up to the altar. The show's about to start. Maybe I should confess everything to him, see if he can cure my haunted self. Get him to hose me down with holy water and set me free.

But I know there's no miracle for me here. Just a moment of peace.

25

I bolt awake. My heart beating hard.

I stare at the glowing red numbers on my alarm clock. Just past two in the morning.

What woke me? Thought I heard something.

I listen to the stillness of the house. Dad's off on night patrol, so there's not even his snoring down the hall to break the quiet.

I wait a few silent heartbeats. I've been so hyperalert, jumping at every little creak. Such a wreck.

But there's nothing now. So I sink back onto my pillow and close my eyes.

Then I hear it again. Sounds like . . . scratching?

Where's that coming from? I listen hard.

It seems so close. Leaning over, I flick on my bedside lamp. I look around.

Scratching, as if there's a cat at my door trying to get in.

Hazy from sleep, I swing out of bed, getting unsteadily to my feet.

Whatever it is, it's louder now. And it's coming from . . . where? I look down.

From the floor?

I stand right over the spot.

Something's scraping at the hardwood from underneath. We've had mice before. But this sounds like something bigger than a mouse.

Am I really awake? Feels like I'm half in a dream.

I crouch down. The scratching stops.

I hold my breath, listening.

The floor creaks under me. Then I catch the slightest movement, just inches from my toes. What's that? A loose board?

I stare at the spot. There it is again—one of the floorboards shifts the tiniest bit. I freeze, unblinking. What the hell?

It's like the foot-long board is bulging out—

creeeee

—rising upward—

eeeeeee

—squealing as it pulls up on its nails.

I'm paralyzed, watching that board come out all the way. Then it topples on its side, leaving a hole in the floor.

I can't be seeing this. I should back away. Go get Mom. Just go.

But I don't. It's like I'm caught in some kind of dream, keeping me here. Slowly, I lean forward to peer into that gap.

So dark down there, where the light barely reaches—

An eye stares back at me. Pressed to the hole.

Screaming, I fall back. I scramble away till I hit the wall.

Wake up! Now!

That's not real. Not real.

I'm shivering so bad I can't stand.

Across the floor I see something move in the gap. Reaching up. Fingers. Muddy fingers, crawling like spider legs. Feeling around the edges of the hole. Searching.

Not real! Go away! Wake up!

There's a cracking sound beside me as my bedroom door opens. I let out another half scream before I see Mom.

"Jane, what's wrong?"

My throat feels choked tight. Takes me a moment before I can speak.

"Jane?"

"S-something's down there."

I point to the hole in the floor.

But it's gone. The board is back in place. Everything looks the same as always.

"What is going on in here?"

"It—it was scratching underneath the floor. And then . . ."

She waits for me to finish, but I can't.

"What, Jane? Is it mice again? Is that it?"

"Didn't you hear anything?"

"Yeah. You screaming the walls down. Scared the life out of me. What's this about?"

I stare at the spot where those fingers came crawling out. Mom's waiting for an answer.

"Maybe it was mice. And maybe a nightmare too."

Mom shivers, hugging herself. "It's freezing in here. You have the window open?"

"No. Must be a draft," I mumble.

Mom heaves a tired sigh, shaking her head. "If it's mice, we'll set some traps out tomorrow. Come sleep with me. You can keep me warm." She reaches out and takes my hand, helping me up. "With your dad on night shift it gets chilly under the sheets."

As she leads me out, I shoot a glance over my shoulder. But the floor is back to normal.

All in my head, I try telling myself. Like those waking dreams Lexi told me about. Please let it be that.

"Your father always squeaks when I push my cold feet up against him in bed," Mom tells me.

"The constable squeaks?"

"Like a startled mouse."

Mom sits down on her bed, blinking her sleepy eyes at me. "After what's happened, I'd be surprised if you weren't having nightmares. But at least you're not out running wild in your sleep."

I shake my head. "I'm nothing but trouble."

I glance at the laptop on her bedside table, with its GPS program running to keep track of me and my ring. Mom always sleeps so deep, she's got the volume on the alarm turned to the max. One time she let me hear what it sounds like, loud enough to wake the dead. I must have let out one hell of a scream to get her up tonight.

"What am I going to do with you, Jane?"

I shrug. "Trade me in? Get a refund? Did you keep my receipt?"

She gives me a drowsy smile. "Catch the light, honey."

Turning it off reluctantly, I get under the covers with her. I feel a little better, not being alone.

I'd feel even safer if Dad still kept his spare gun in the drawers beside the bed. Since I started sleepwalking he has it locked away.

But what am I thinking?

Can't shoot a nightmare.

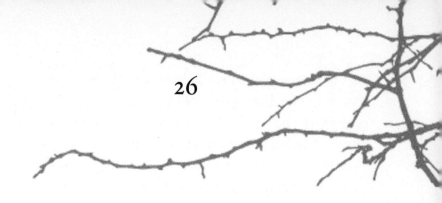

26

At breakfast it's like dawn of the dead. Me and Dad are both sleepy zombies. I'm nodding off into my cereal, and after his night shift the constable's about to use his pancakes for a pillow.

I jump awake when I feel something sticking in my ear. Pulling away, I whip my head around.

Mom's leaning in close, holding an ear thermometer in her hand.

"What the hell?"

"Relax," she says. "Just taking your temperature."

"How about a little warning?"

"Well, you bitch and moan every time I ask."

She writes down my temp in her notebook.

If Mom's not monitoring my meds, temperature or my migraines, she's thinking up sneaky ways to test my hand-eye coordination.

Like last week when I kept misplacing my keys, and she would find them and toss them to me. "Catch!" When I caught them she'd give me a little nod. It took me a few days to realize that she was hiding my keys to give her a chance to check my motor skills.

I know she's just watching out for me, and I feel bad about what I've put her and Dad through. But I make a grouchy patient.

Dad's trying to chew and yawn at the same time. It ain't pretty.

"How was the graveyard shift?" I ask.

"Cold, wet and nasty. We had three crashes. People don't know how to drive in the rain."

"So, any word yet about those bones you found?" I ask.

"The forensics unit determined that the remains are caucasian, not Indian. So it isn't from any native burial. Now we're checking dental records on old missing children cases," Dad says. "They've narrowed the age to twelve or thirteen."

"That's too horrible," Mom says. "Makes my heart hurt just thinking about it. Left out there and forgotten."

"They find out how it died?" I ask.

"Oh, I can't listen to this." Mom gets up. "No morgue talk in the morning. That's a new rule." She leaves the kitchen.

Dad squints his bloodshot eyes at me. "Why do you want to know about that?"

I shrug. "Can't get it out of my head. I was there when you spotted it. Come on, I grew up on cop talk. I can handle it."

He rubs the fallen bridge of his busted nose, like he does when he's deciding things. "Yeah, I guess you can. They did the autopsy. The cause of death is blunt force trauma. There was a severe fracture to the back of the skull."

For a second I flash back on that skull in the mud. The jaws open wide, trying to breathe, or scream. I push the image away.

"So that's how it died," I say.

"He. It was a boy."

"Any way to tell how long it—he's—been buried there?"

"If I'd known there was going to be a breakfast interrogation, I'd have brought my notes. The forensics unit is trying to narrow down the time frame. Right now, they're thinking he's been in the ground a decade at least. We're still waiting for fiber analysis on the remnants of clothes they found with the bones. That might give us a better idea."

"How about the DNA?"

"That takes time. The lab is testing a sample from the remains. We'll see if they get a match in the database."

"How hard is it going to be to identify him? I mean, are there a lot of unsolved missing-kid cases?"

"Nationally, there are about fifty thousand kids reported missing every year. Most are found pretty quick. Some turn up on their own, others are runaways or parental abduction cases. But some stay lost. Too many."

Dad gets up.

"So are we done?" he asks. "Interrogation over? Am I free to go?"

I nod. "For now. But don't leave town."

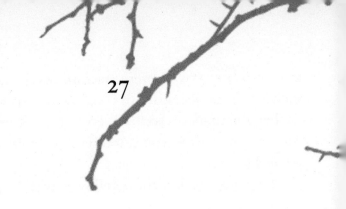

27

Nowhere is safe anymore. Can't even hide away at home, in my own room.

This used to be a safe place, the Blushing Rose. Peaceful, quiet—maybe dull. But never dark and creepy.

Now I can't be here by myself. I help out when Mom's around. She's working the counter while I'm in back. I can hear her talking with a customer about tulip bulbs.

I'm potting African violets, mixing worm castings in with the soil. Violets love worm poo, makes them really—

Tap tap tap.

I drop the pot, spinning toward the sound of—

Tap tap tap. Knocking at the alley door.

"Delivery," a voice calls from the other side. Ryan.

I exhale, shaking my head. I am such a wreck.

Rushing to let him in, I take a quick peek in the mirror over the sink. My big startled eyes stare back. My hair is wild as weeds. I try to fix that mess, getting worm stuff in it. Giving up, I go open the door.

"Hi, Ryan."

His hair is wet from the rain, streaks of mud and soil on his cheeks like war paint. As big a mess as me. But smiling through the dirt.

"Hey, Jane. I've got a little bit of everything for you today. I even brought the sun."

He hands me a potted sunflower, with bright yellow petals the color of summer.

Ryan starts unloading from the truck while I make space in the back room. It's a tight fit, with us brushing past each other. I try not to say much, keeping it all business.

When he's done, we check the order sheet.

"I miss anything?" he asks.

"No. Perfect." I look at the sheet, at the new plants crowding us together, everywhere but at him.

"How have you been, Jane? I mean, is your recovery going okay?"

I open my mouth to say some easy lie, like that I'm improving, getting better. But I can't. "Don't know. Still breathing, anyway."

"That's a good sign. But you look kind of beat."

I meet his eyes for a split second but force myself to break away.

"I am kind of beat. Real tired. Not sleeping good."

"Gotta get your rest. Sleep's a great healer," he says. "Can I give you something?"

I feel a blush heating my cheeks and turn around to rearrange some pots so he doesn't see. "Um . . . what did you have in mind?"

"Hold on. I'll show you." He goes out in the alley, and a minute later he's back with a plant. "*Cestrum nocturnum. Night-blooming jasmine.*"

The plant's small flowers are bright white and star-shaped. "Is this more of your mystic medicine?"

"It's pure science. Aromatherapy. You inhale the scent molecules into your lungs; they get absorbed into your blood and flow to your brain. Jasmine is best for calming and easing anxiety, headaches. Lets you relax and breathe easy. The flowers release their scent at night, so they'll help you sleep."

"Thanks," I mumble, taking the plant from him. "I can use the help. I'll give it a try."

"Let me know," Ryan says, brushing the hair from his eyes and adding a new streak of dirt to his forehead.

Following him to the door, I watch him get in the truck. I hate treating Ryan coldly. Making him think I'm not interested, don't care, don't want him. I hate it so much I can't stop myself from calling out.

"So what are you, some kind of witch doctor on wheels? What else have you got in there? Magic potions? Miracle cures?"

"Whatever you need, I've got." Ryan smiles, leaning out the window. "The name of your flower—jasmine—it's Persian. Means 'queen of the night.' Just let her work her magic on you."

I give him a little wave and watch my medicine man drive off into the drizzly afternoon.

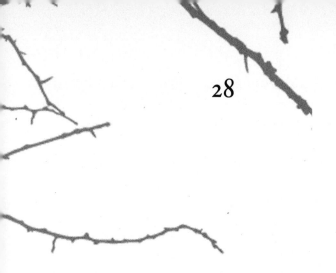

28

I'm trying not to stare at the guy sitting across from me in the waiting room of the CT scan clinic.

This appointment got me the day off from school, but I'd rather be stuck in some mind-numbing math class than here. Mom dropped me off between flower deliveries. She was going to stay with me, but that would just make me more tense, so I told her I'd call her after to pick me up.

I flip through an old *People* magazine, but my gaze drifts back to the red-haired guy.

He seems to be napping. Slouched down in the chair. He's wearing a black hooded sweatshirt and jeans. The guy is skeleton skinny, with twiggy wrists sticking out of his sleeves. Under the hood, I can see his caved-in cheeks and scrawny neck. The angles of his face stand out sharp beneath the flesh. He looks young, like he's thirteen, maybe. But something's wrong with him. That's why he's here, I guess.

The woman sitting beside him—his mother?—is

focused on a crossword puzzle. She's hooked up to a portable oxygen tank on wheels, the tubes stuck in her nostrils. What a family!

I shift in my seat to keep my butt from falling asleep.

The door to the scan room opens and the technician pokes his head out.

"Mrs. Garcia? We're ready for you now."

Crossword lady gets up and follows him inside.

But the guy in the sweatshirt doesn't budge. She says nothing to him and never looks back. Not her son, then? Guess he's got his own appointment with the scanner.

I check my watch for the twentieth time. The seconds crawl by. I toss the magazine back on the table, and I'm reaching for another when a sudden migraine flares through my brain, with a shock that makes me gasp. I lean forward, holding my head. It's like somebody's hammering that nail deeper.

I fumble in my jacket for my pills.

Dry-swallowing one of the migraine busters, I try to breathe slowly and wait for it to work. I'm staring at the floor when a loud buzzing sound fills my ears. A side effect of the headaches.

Just gotta ride it out. It'll pass.

I glance over at the guy. He's awake, watching me from under his hood. His eyes catch me. They're such a strange shade—pale amber. A shock of color in that gray face. Holding the look for just a moment, I break away before it gets weird.

I close my eyes as the buzzing surrounds me. I try

covering my ears to block it out. That's when I hear something past the white noise.

Something . . . like a voice! Coming from inside my head. I strain to make it out. I can almost—

Jane.

My breath stops in my throat. What was that?

Jane.

I press my palms tight against my ears, blocking out everything but what's coming from inside.

You're mine, Jane.

The same voice from my nightmare—buried in the coffin.

You're mine. Mine. Mine.

It echoes in me.

Don't make me hurt you
make me hurt you
make me hurt

"Jane?"

I jump in my seat, my eyes flying open. The technician is standing by the door.

"What? What?" I say, looking around the room.

The sick guy is gone. Where did he go? How long have I been sitting here like this? Lost in my own head.

"We're ready for your scan now."

The buzzing is gone. I hear him clearly. And the pain is passing, eased by the pill.

Where did the voice come from?

I get up shakily and follow the technician.

Jumpy and distracted, I half listen as he runs through the CT scan procedure with me.

What was with that creepy guy out there? Where did he go? And how long was I out of it? Felt like only a minute.

I wince as the tech sticks an IV in my arm, injecting the dye that will make the veins in my brain stand out on the imaging.

"Lie down now. The scan will take about ten minutes. Just try to relax. I need you to keep completely still while we're running the test."

The scanner is a big blocky thing with a doughnut hole in the middle, and they load you in like a human torpedo. I get up on the tray and lie back, staring at the ceiling, while the technician goes in the next room to fire it up.

That sick guy couldn't have gone in for his scan before me. I wasn't zoned out for that long. Was I?

The tray shudders into motion, sliding me into the glowing white mouth of the scanner.

As tests go, this one is painless. But it can drive you nuts, to have to keep perfectly motionless for so long with nothing to look at but the roof of the tube. Gets claustrophobic quick if you let it.

The scan starts up with a deep humming sound. I shut my eyes, trying to relax. Which is impossible.

My mind is going a mile a minute, replaying, *You're mine. Don't make me hurt you.*

What's that supposed to mean? I don't get—

The scanner's hum cuts off suddenly into silence.

We done already?

I open my eyes to darkness.

What is this? Power outage? Can't see a thing. You'd think with all the radiation this monster throws off it would glow in the dark.

I wait for the lights to come back on.

"Hello," I call out. "Anybody there?"

Nothing. Where's the panic button?

"Little help," I try louder. "I'm kind of stuck in here."

Seconds tick by. Did the tech go on a break or something?

After a minute I decide, Screw it! I'm getting out. I put my hands up to try to push myself back out.

But my fingers hit something cold and damp. It crumbles under my touch, breaking apart and showering down on my face. I swipe it away. What the hell is this?

I press my palms against the walls of the scanner.

They aren't there. It feels more like—

Earth. My fingertips sink into it. Reaching under me, I discover more dirt.

I'm losing it! This is not happening!

"Hey!" I yell into the blackness.

My voice is deadened, absorbed by these dirt walls.

The roof is so low I can't sit up, can only move inches in any direction. Contorting my right arm, I stretch it past my head and find empty space. Like I'm in some kind of tunnel.

No! This is not real! I'm in the hospital clinic. Safe.

But my body's not listening—my heart's racing, legs shaking, I'm starting to hyperventilate.

Raising my head up till it hits the hard-packed earth

above me, I stare down the length of my body, straining to see.

There! What's that? I see a little spark of light. Two lights, getting bigger.

I don't even blink. Don't want to lose sight of them.

"I'm here!" I call. "Over here!"

I focus on the sparks as they come closer.

"Get me out of—" I start to shout.

But now I make out what those lights are.

Eyes. Shining amber eyes.

And in the glow they cast, I make out a face.

It's the guy from the waiting room, crawling toward me.

You're mine.

I feel a stab of panic, like an injection of ice water straight to my heart.

Mine.

No! No! No!

Those eyes are on fire, closing in.

I claw at the dirt surrounding me. Gotta get out. Squirming back. Inch by inch. But the walls are caving in. Earth crashing down. Burying me.

I suck in a breath. Dirt in my mouth.

Something cold clamps around my ankle. I kick out frantically.

Then an icy hand grabs my knee with frozen fingers. Dragging me back.

No—

My eyes fly open. Light! Blinding white light. A stranger's face looming over me.

"You okay?"

I can't speak. Struggling for oxygen.

"Calm down," says the technician with a worried frown. "You fell asleep. That's all."

I sit up fast. Too fast. My head pounds with a dizzy rush.

"Take it slow. Some people doze off in there. It happens."

I've got the shakes. Shooting a glance over my shoulder, I see the scanner with its doughnut-hole tube.

No tunnel. No darkness. No eyes.

The tech gives me a reassuring smile.

"Bad dream?" he asks.

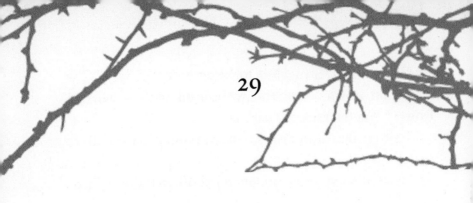

29

"Tell me I'm not crazy."

"You want me to lie?" Lexi says.

"Be serious."

We're sitting in Shipwrecks Cafe. After my bad trip in the scanner, I called Lexi and she skipped her last class to meet up.

"Sorry," she says. "Okay, seriously. Don't panic. Maybe it was one of those waking dreams, that hypnagogia thing I told you about. You're stressed, zapped with migraines, going on no sleep and full of pharmaceuticals. That's a monster mess screwing with your brain. So maybe when you closed your eyes for a second, you snapped right into a nightmare. Doesn't make you a nutcase."

I gulp my coffee, trying to warm up, and trying to believe her explanation. I'm drinking decaf, since my nerves are already fried.

We're sitting by the windows, leaning on the old counter with all those initials and hearts carved into it— the love log. Outside the wind is buffeting the glass. The café is filled, and it's good to be in a crowd, safer. The jazzy music and the general noise insulate us so nobody can overhear.

"What about that sick guy in the waiting room?" I ask.

"You sure you've never seen him before?"

"A total stranger. I'd remember those eyes."

"Maybe your brain just spliced him into your scanner nightmare. He was fresh in your mind."

That sounds kind of weak. But I'll grab onto anything to keep from going under. Because I'm starting to think it was more than just some bones that got unearthed in the landslide. Like something else was uncovered with them and set free to haunt me.

"But I wasn't dreaming the voice. I was wide awake in the waiting room when I heard it."

She shrugs. "I don't know. This has gone way past weird."

We stare out at the rain. January is the grayest month here.

Lexi sips her coffee. "I found something on those near-death-experience websites that might fit in with what you went through when you were flatlining. When your shadow took you away. There are these things called *Grim Enders*."

"What're they?"

"Souls who don't cross over into the light."

I hug my arms close, trying to get warm. "Why don't they?"

"Some say that they just can't see the light. Like

they're blind to it. Some think they're scared of the light, or they're sure it won't take them. So they get trapped in *The Divide*."

"The what?"

"The Divide. It's this dark nothing kind of place that separates the living world from the *other side*—the afterlife. It's where you end up if you can't, or won't, go to the light."

"I never knew there was this whole geography to the afterlife."

I can tell Lexi's been chatting online with those Second Chance people. Death tourists, who were "just visiting" the other side.

"There are a lot of different descriptions of the Divide. They say for most departing souls who cross over, the Divide is just a borderline that's as thin as a thread. But for some it's like the Grand Canyon, darkness stretching to infinity, the end of everything. And it swallows them up."

"Grim Enders." The wind rattles the window, trying to find a way in.

"They're condemned to the dark because they can't face the light. No afterlife for them. No nothing. Just this sad and lonely sort of hell. That's their eternity." Lexi digs in her pocket and hands over a folded sheet of paper. "I got this off one of the sites."

I smooth it out on the counter.

It's an illustration, with a caption that says *Grim Enders at the Gate*. It shows a glowing moonlike "gate" to the other side, surrounded by darkness, and a ghostly woman in a nightgown with long hair about to step through it. But all around the edges of this gate black creatures are hanging there like gargoyles. The light dies on these things, leaving them as faceless shadows. They reach out, dark fingers brushing over the woman's hair and tugging at her gown.

"Has anyone had a close encounter with these Enders?"

Lexi nods. "It's pretty rare, but there are reports of them lurking in the Divide to spy on the souls crossing into the light. And when the near-death people are brought back to life, on their return trip to their bodies, they say the Enders cry out to them. Sometimes even touch them as they pass by."

I know that touch. When my shadow in the emergency room ripped me away from the light it left an invisible tattoo, in the shape of its fingers.

"You think that's what my shadow really is? One of these Enders?" I look at the picture with the dark creatures that seem dead to the light.

"Kind of matches your description. But they're supposed to be powerless. They can't attack you. They're trapped in the Divide. They don't try to steal you away and don't follow you home."

But somehow my Grim Ender did.

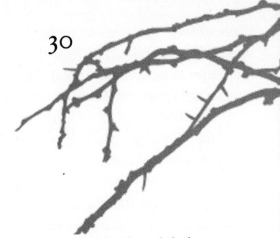

30

This is Lexi's idea. A day off from death and darkness.

"You need a break," she told me on the phone this misty Saturday morning. "Before you have a breakdown."

She's right. I need to forget everything for an afternoon and try to find my way back to the real world.

So here we are at the mall.

"I've got the perfect cure for you," she says as we step inside. "Let's try a little white-trash spa."

I smile. Exactly what I need. By "spa" she means a mall crawl, where we go around the stores trying out cosmetics and perfumes, giving ourselves makeovers and collecting samples, and skimming magazines in the bookstore.

I'm doing it all in kind of a daze, so sleep deprived it feels like a sweet, silly dream.

Then we take photos of us trying on clothes we're not going to buy, from ultrasleek to dead skanky. Everything looks good on Lexi; she's got a petite hourglass figure. But me—flat, no hips and no bounce in my butt. People see me and think tomboy. If only they knew what was hiding in my room—wallpapered in half-naked guys, my library of lust in the closet.

After the crawl, we end our spa at the food court, in a peaceful spot near the fake waterfall, eating nachos and curly fries.

I say no to seeing a movie. I'm not up to sitting in the dark for two hours, constantly looking over my shoulder.

I feel safe in this crowd, under the bright lights. So relaxed I could curl up for a catnap next to those plastic palms. I try to focus on what Lexi's saying.

"Look at this shirt. My mom keeps stealing my stuff from the laundry. It's all stretched out by her big boobs. She says people think we're sisters when they see us together, which is completely delusional. . . ."

Her voice gets lost in the background noise of falling water. I nod, closing my eyes for a second.

Snorting awake, I look around, disoriented. Then I notice Lexi filming me across the table.

"How long was I . . . ?"

"Just ten minutes." She sets her camera down. "Thought I'd let you rest a while. You know you get all twitchy in your sleep? Like a dog who dreams he's running."

I stretch my back with a groan. "If I see that online I'll use your guts for garters."

She laughs. "So are you up for a drive? I was thinking of taking some video for my rain flick. Perfect weather."

"Sure. Where to?"

* * *

Widows' Peak is the highest point on this stretch of coast. It looks down on Edgewood and all the way over to the cliffs of Lookout Hill on the far side of town. The two rises stick out from the old forest that surrounds the town, bookending the place.

"How does this thing work?" I ask Lexi.

She's got me helping with the sound, using the directional microphone she borrowed from her film club.

"You just aim it and press Record. Wear the earbuds so you hear what you're catching. And don't worry, it's waterproof."

We're parked at the end of the gravel road that leads to the peak. Getting out of the car, I stick the buds in and pull up the hood of my yellow slicker. Lexi looks more than ever like the Reaper's little sister, with her hood hiding her face and her black slicker reaching down to her ankles.

A heavy drizzle is falling, but I can still see pretty far. The view from here is why the fishermen's wives and mothers came to this peak. They could look out to sea, trying to spot the fishing boats with their husbands and sons coming home. But for the ones who never made it back, the widows kept watch till all hope was lost. I can just make out the tips of the Teeth, the jagged spine of reefs that's been chewing through boat hulls for over a century.

Experimenting with the microphone, I wander around capturing rain sounds. The mike magnifies everything, turning the drops into drumbeats. The rain patters like hail on the car roof, crackles in the leaf-stripped bushes, sizzles off the rocks.

Standing by the edge of the peak, I aim down to where the surf is breaking on the rocks. The waves roar in my ears, loud and wild, making my heart pound.

This close to shore the wind mixes the drizzle with the crashing surf, so the rain picks up a salty taste, like tears. I lick it off my lips.

Gusts make the drops hiss as they hit the microphone.

Lexi's filming a little waterfall created by the downpour, running off the peak. She's collecting shots to add to her *thousand words for rain*. There are so many ways of saying it—from cloudbursts to torrents, flooders, soakers and drenchers. Drowned dog days and weeping nights.

What's falling on us right now is called a Pineapple Express. That's when a storm comes all the way from Hawaii, filling up on the warm waters of the South Pacific and dumping it on the coast here.

I head back to the car before I get washed over the edge.

Shutting out the rain, I check my cell phone and find new texts from Mom. The usual stuff: *where R U? what U up 2? how U feelin?* I text her back: *me + Lexi nowhere special, feeling fine.*

Mom probably knows exactly where I am. She's been tracking the GPS in my cell since I refused to wear my magic ring everywhere.

Flicking through the photos on my phone, I see shots of me and Lexi from our fashion show today. Her looking hot, me not. Then I find two pictures of Ryan that I dug up way back before I got nailed. One is from the digital yearbook on the website of his high school, up the coast in Heron's Landing, where he graduated last year. It's a standard academic mug shot. The other pic is from the greenhouse site, showing him holding a basketful of hothouse tomatoes, with a big ridiculous smile.

Maybe we could have been something.

I've got the night-blooming jasmine he gave me on my bedside table, filling the air with soothing scent molecules.

When Lexi joins me I'm drying out with the heat on and the stereo blasting. She tosses her slicker in back and rubs her hands in the rush of warm air from the vent.

"Where now?" she shouts over the music.

"Nowhere."

She's okay with that. So we ease the seats back, putting our feet up on the dash. The stereo's so loud I can't hear myself think. And I like it.

Forgetting everything. Breathing easy for a while.

31

"Quick, turn on your TV," Lexi tells me when I answer my phone. I just got home from our spa day an hour ago.

"Why? What's—"

"Channel nine. Quick!"

"Okay, calm down." I flick on the little TV on top of my dresser. "Now, what am I looking at?"

"Just watch."

It's the six o'clock news. A woman wearing sunglasses is standing on the lawn in front of a house, with a bunch of microphones aimed at her. She's leaning on a bearded man who's got his arm around her shoulders.

"I thought not knowing was worse than anything," she says, her voice cracking. "But now we've lost him all over again. We never gave up hope. It was all we had. Now there's just . . . nothing."

The caption at the bottom of the screen reads *PARENTS OF MURDERED BOY.*

The woman starts to break down. "I'm sorry . . . I can't . . ." She turns from the camera sobbing, and the man leads her toward the house.

The picture cuts to a reporter. "This afternoon the parents of Leo Gage were notified that the remains found last week after a landslide in Edgewood were positively identified as their son. It was eighteen years ago that Leo went missing. Back then he was just thirteen years old when he was last seen on a sunny September day in this small coastal town of Ferny."

His picture fills the screen. A grinning red-head, with *amber* eyes. My heart skips a beat.

He's the guy from the hospital clinic, from my nightmare in the scanner. He's not painfully thin and sickly in the picture, like when I saw him. But I'm sure.

My knees go shaky and I sit down on the foot of my bed.

"Hey, you still with me?"

I jump at the faraway voice coming from the phone in my lap. Oh, Lexi.

"That's him," I tell her.

"Yeah. They identified the body with dental records."

"No. I mean, that's the guy I saw at the clinic yesterday."

There's a long silence on her end.

On the TV they're showing old footage of the original search from years ago. Cops and volunteers combing the woods. Dogs trying to pick up the scent.

"You sure?" Lexi asks finally.

"Yeah."

"Wow. That's just . . ."

The screen shows the MISSING poster of Leo Gage.

"This is deeply weird," Lexi says.

Below his photo on the poster, his height, weight and description are listed. And at the bottom it reads:

Last seen wearing a black hooded sweatshirt, blue jeans and black rain boots.

What he was wearing at the hospital.

Leo Gage.

Unbelievable. As they show the interview with the grieving mother again, I realize she looks familiar too somehow. And that blue house behind her.

I've seen that place somewhere.

But how? Where? The memory stays teasingly out of reach.

I focus on the house. It almost feels like I've been there. Been inside.

I gasp.

"You okay, Jane?"

I can't speak.

Because I know where I've seen that woman, and her blue house. It was when I died and my shadow came for me. Sharing its memories, showing me pieces of its life.

His life. This dead guy. Leo Gage.

It was him! He was waiting for me when I flatlined.

"Jane, can you hear me?" Lexi asks.

I try to find my voice.

"Jane? What's wrong?"

"Everything," I say. "He's my shadow."

32

Me and Lexi sit in front of her computer watching a stranger's home movies.

After they identified his body yesterday, Leo's story has been all over the news. They keep playing footage from when he disappeared. Interviews with the parents, their pleas to whoever took their son to let him go. Candlelight vigils held in a nearby park. Neighbors tying blue ribbons for Leo Gage around trees, street signs and mailboxes.

And then there are these movies. Heartbreaking stuff from when he was a kid. Leo in his pajamas on Christmas morning, with his hair sticking up from bed, knee-deep in torn gift wrappings. Sunburned at the beach, carrying a shovel and pail. Bouncing on a trampoline. All happy and hyper. Then, when he's older, skateboarding in the driveway and wiping out.

Leo Gage. My shadow has a name. I'm trying to wrap my head around that.

I went sleepless last night, coming to grips with all of

this. Lexi's been helping me piece it together. It's great having an insomniac best friend, on call at all hours.

So here's what we figured out—

Leo has been with me for a long time. Since I was little. Watching and waiting to take me down.

But now he's not hiding in my shadow anymore. I saw him at the clinic, heard his voice. I'm sure he was that *thing* breaking out of the cooler at the shop and scratching under the floorboards of my room.

But who knows why he chose *me* to haunt for all these years?

And I never really lost him, when they brought me back from the dead and I broke away. I didn't leave him behind.

It's as if on my return trip to the living after I got nailed, the gate to the other side got left open a crack, setting him free. So he's not just a shadow now—he's a real *ghost*.

And he's gotten stronger. Before, my shadow would manipulate my body to make me hurt myself. But on the night of the landslide it stretched beyond the limits of my flesh, reaching out to where those remains lay buried, bringing the hillside crashing down.

Then I realized something else when I was thinking about the familiar stretch of road that got buried in the slide. The place was so familiar to me because that was where Constable Granger found me walking the center line in my sleep. And that's not the only time they caught me wandering unconscious on that road. It's like I was always headed there.

Everybody has a theory about why I've been sleep-walking. Mom thinks it means I want to run away. Dad calls it a death wish. The doctor says it's a side effect of my brain injury. But they're wrong—I'm sure of it now.

It's been my shadow all along. He led me to that spot, near his hidden grave. I just know it. Maybe so he could bring that hill down on me and bury me with him. Or maybe he was trying to get me run over on the way. But my shadow is behind my sleepwalking.

It wants me dead. I just don't know why.

"Want some?" Lexi asks, offering me the bowl of pop-corn she's been munching on.

"It's not really popcorn kind of viewing for me."

"I know. It's just that I eat when I'm nervous. Or freaked out."

"You're freaked? I just found out a dead guy's been haunting me since I was a kid."

On the screen, Leo's laughing and wrestling with the family dog. I shake my head. That's not the ghost I know—the dark thing he's changed into.

Watching him, I feel a familiar shudder squirming up my spine.

Glancing back quickly, I find only empty air.

But I can sense it right now. My shadow. *Him.* In the room with us. So close. Like he's peering over my shoul-der to watch these scenes from his life.

"You okay?" Lexi asks.

"No. I'm not."

"What's wrong?"

"It's here. He's here."

"Him?" Lexi frowns; then her eyebrows shoot up. She points to the guy on the screen.

I nod.

"Here in the room?"

"Yeah."

"Where?"

"Behind me."

"No way." She gets up to take a look around, sees nothing. "So. What do we do?"

I just shake my head. What can I do?

"But it only ever hurts you if you piss it off, right? I mean, if you . . . cheat on it."

"I—I haven't done anything like that."

I'm not telling just Lexi, but my ghost too. I've been playing by its rules. Why won't it leave me alone?

"Maybe it's just trying to scare you, then, like it's been doing lately. Just . . . here to haunt you or whatever. You ever try talking to it? To him?"

"Just when I tell him to go away and leave me alone."

"How about if I give it a try?"

"What for?"

"Can't hurt, right?"

I shrug. "Okay, I guess."

"All right. How do I start?" She thinks about it a moment. "Um, Leo? You there?" She waits for an answer. "Can you maybe give us a sign you're here? Anything? Flick the lights or something?"

Silence.

"He doesn't do tricks," I tell her.

"Right. Okay, then. How about we get to the main

question? What do you want?" She pauses. Silence. "If you want something, you've got to let us know somehow."

Not a whisper.

I don't like this. We should stop.

"Why are you so stuck on Jane?"

I'm about to say "Quit it" when my thoughts start to go fuzzy. There's a buzzing in my head.

No, stop! I try to speak, but my voice won't work. Don't!

My head's spinning, and I almost fall off the chair. He's taking control. Can't fight it.

My left hand moves in my lap. I look down, watching it like it belongs to someone else. Then its shadow stretches up, reaching over to Lexi's desk, dragging my fingers along with it. I don't know what it's going for till it grabs a pen. There's a spiral-bound notebook beside the keyboard. My hand comes to rest on top of a page of Lexi's notes.

Holding the pen tight in my fist, my hand starts scratching at the paper.

"What are you doing?" Lexi's standing right next to me, but she sounds so far away.

Something's taking shape on the page. The rapid strokes are sketching a dark figure in black ink.

"Jane, you still with me?" She passes her hand in front of my eyes, but I keep drawing. "Don't screw around."

I can't answer.

"What is that?" Lexi leans in to look. "A bird?"

A bird? Yes. That's it. Coming into focus now—wings

stretched out, a curved beak, the feet ending in claws. Maybe a crow.

"Jane, come on. Say something."

My voice is lost. No words will come.

"Leo?" she tries. "Is that you?"

I lean on the pen too heavy, ripping the paper as I slash three lines beside the crow, making a Υ.

"Υ? Yes? Is that a yes?"

I retrace the letter, tearing deeper.

"Hold on." Lexi lifts my hand so she can turn to a new page.

I start filling the fresh paper with a rough square, sketching a shallow triangle on top. I dig at the page, darkening the outline, then making a small rectangle standing inside the square. Like a door.

"A house?" Lexi guesses.

My hand pauses, then slashes another Υ.

"Your house, Leo?"

N

I go back to the sketch, drawn cartoon-simple, and start inking it in. Turning the house black. I add something on the top, scrawling curved lines sticking up from opposite sides of the roof, each ending in a point, making what looks like horns.

A house with horns.

"Whose house?" Lexi presses. "Did something bad happen there?"

Υ

My strokes are getting more agitated with her

questions, tearing through the page. She lifts my hand again and turns to a fresh one.

"What happened? What bad thing?"

My fist is shaking, the knuckles gone white.

"Is that . . . where you died?"

I carve three long slashes across the page. Then I go over them, making them deeper. Deeper.

Υ

Υ

Υ

Ripping and shredding through. A wild swipe sends the notebook flying off the desk.

"Okay, enough! Stop it!"

But I can't. I keep going, scraping into the desktop.

Υ

Υ

Υ

"Jane, wake up now. Wake! Up!" I feel Lexi shaking my shoulder. "Snap out of it!"

Lexi makes a grab for the pen. But I'm too quick. I watch my fist pull away from her, rising up high and then plunging down. Stabbing the pen into my right wrist.

I feel only a faint sting through my numb haze. When my hand pulls up again, blood spills out of the hole I've made on the inside of my wrist. I try another stab, but Lexi catches me. We struggle, and our skulls crack together. I lose my grip on the pen.

And it's like the lights come back on inside my head, burning off the fog. The pain hits me then.

Blood runs down my palm, dripping off my fingers. Deep red.

"Jane? You there?" Lexi stares at me like I'm a stranger.

"Yeah," I gasp through my teeth. "I'm here."

My blood spatters the notebook lying on the floor, staining the pages.

Painting that black house red.

33

Down in the basement, I'm doing laundry. Just trying to keep busy and act normal, as if nothing's wrong, like that will make it true. But it does calm me a little, this every-day stuff.

Our basement is a jungle of old junk. Boxes stacked high and forgotten. The ground-level window above lets in a gray wash of light from the stormy day.

I'm tossing the load in the dryer. I try to do it one-handed, with my right wrist still stinging from where I stabbed myself.

Lexi freaked at all the blood and wanted to get me to the emergency room. But the wound wasn't that deep. And I'm so sick of hospitals. Besides, that would mean too many questions. How was I going to explain it? So we got me cleaned up, carefully, and Nurse Lexi bandaged my wrist. I just have to stick to long sleeves for a while and hide it from my parents. They can't help me with what's happening anyway. Can't protect me.

I remember taking Dad's self-defense course for women over at the community center. It was a police outreach kind of thing, where he showed us all the moves—kicks, punches, eye gouges, scratches, how to stab with a nail file and claw with your keys. I know how to fight back, but I can't hit something that isn't even there.

Lexi's feeling so guilty, like it was her fault because she tried interrogating my ghost, making him mad. She's texting me every ten minutes, checking to make sure I'm okay. And we've been trying to figure out what it all means. Piecing together my vision of the bald man and the crow with my drawings of the bird and the black house with horns.

I slam the dryer shut and set it for a half hour. As it starts up, the lights dim. We get a lot of brownouts during windstorms.

I can hear it gusting outside now. Looking up at the small window, I feel a draft brush past me with a hushed sound.

I turn to go.

Someone's sitting on the stairs.

It's him! The hood of his sweatshirt is pulled up, shadowing his face, so all I see are his eyes, shining amber.

I back up into some boxes and grab for whatever I can use as a weapon. I find a golf club and hold it out in front of me.

"Get away from me!"

He doesn't move. Just watches. He looks so real and solid sitting there.

"What? What do you want?"

He stares into me, those eyes burning bright.

You.

I recoil at the voice in my head. He's ten feet from me, but it's like his lips are pressed to my ear.

"Why? Why me? What did I do?"

There's a long silence, with nothing but the rumble of the dryer and the drum of my heartbeat.

It was always you.

"Leave me alone. Go! Away!"

He just sits there blocking my escape.

My sweaty palms are slick on the handle of the club. I'm so scared, and so sick of being scared. I have to try something.

"I know who you are. Leo Gage."

Those eyes flare with yellow fire.

"I know something bad happened to you."

He steps down the stairs to the basement floor.

"M-maybe if you tell me, I can help."

No!

What am I doing? I don't want to make this thing angry. I know what it's capable of. But what else can I do?

"Just try. P-please. Tell me . . . tell me about the bald man with the bird."

SHUT UP!

His voice is deafening inside my skull. I try to back away, but I'm cornered against the boxes.

His eyes blaze so bright it hurts to look at them.

Come with me. I'll make it quick. Then we can stay together.

I'm shaking so badly I can't even speak.

I feel him reaching out to me. Into me. And—

A squealing sound cuts through the air. The basement

door opens above on its creaky hinges and a stream of light spills down the stairs.

"Jane?" Mom calls. "You down there?"

I gasp like I'm waking up, sucking in a deep breath.

Spinning around, I scan the basement. Nothing. I'm alone.

"Jane?"

It takes me a second to get my voice back. "Yeah. I'm here."

"Phone for you. It's Lexi."

My rubbery legs barely hold me up.

"You coming?" she asks.

"Yeah."

"Don't forget we have a doctor's appointment later." Mom walks away, and I want to yell, Wait for me!

I move while she's still within earshot. Quick! Before he comes back.

Stumbling up the stairs, I trip, but don't fall. I slam the door shut behind me, leaning against the wall and stare at the doorknob as if it's going to start turning any second.

When it doesn't, I go down the hall and pick up the phone with trembling hands.

"Lexi?"

"Hey, Jane, I found it!"

So good to hear her voice right now. Something to hold on to. I take a steadying breath.

"Found what?"

"A house with horns."

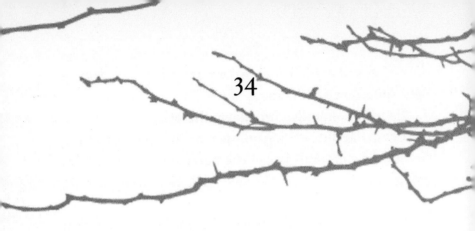

34

The nail has to come out.

Dr. Simon, my neurologist, just broke the news. Me, Mom and Dad sit facing him in his office.

"The risk factors of not extracting it are too great," he says, showing us why on his computer. "The main concern is blood flow. The nail is lodged here in the cerebrum, right next to the medial occipital artery and a number of smaller blood vessels. While it hasn't shifted, the surrounding scar tissue continues to build up, putting pressure on these vessels. Even a minor blockage could be dangerous."

"Dangerous how?" Mom asks.

"It could possibly cause a stroke, or brain-cell atrophy if the area is starved for blood. And because this region is part of the visual cortex, her sight could be affected."

The image on the screen is from my latest scan. It shows my brain colored in bright blues and greens, with a small area of orange. The nail itself is black and has these dark streaks radiating out from it, as if it's shining with some black light.

"Why does the nail look like that?" I ask. "What's with those lines sticking out of it?"

"Metallic objects can cause a distortion in the imaging. This is called an aliasing effect. It's what gives the nail that glow. The darker blue around it is the scar tissue, which has grown incrementally with each new scan we take."

"And this orange patch here." I lean over to point it out. "Does that mean anything?"

"That just indicates a spike in brain activity during the scan, in your visual cortex. Could be caused by a bright light."

No, it wasn't a light. That's what my brain looks like when I'm seeing *him*. When I had my freakout in the scanner.

"How soon can we get this done, then?" Dad asks.

"I've already consulted with a neurosurgeon. He's available later this week, and the operation can be performed right here at Mercy."

Dr. Simon runs through the operation with us. Real horror-movie stuff. Sawing off a portion of my skull to dig the nail out, cleaning away the scar tissue. The whole procedure takes about eight hours.

Mom's taking notes. She and Dad grill the doc. I'm not really listening to all the details. Don't tell me how, just do it! I'm ready.

I know, my haunting started way before I got nailed. So I'm not fooling myself that this surgery is going to cure me of my ghost.

But I'm hoping it might put Leo back to sleep. He left

me alone for years between the train and the nail gun. He let me live.

But with the nail in me he seems stronger somehow. I can see him, hear him. It's almost like that sliver of metal is keeping the gate between this world and the great beyond open.

So cut it out. And slam that gate shut. Send him back to hiding in my shadow and buy me some time to figure out how to get rid of him permanently.

There must be a way. Now that I know who he really is—or was. If I can find out what happened to him, maybe I've got a chance. We're getting closer, me and Lexi. She found a house with horns.

Not a house, really. Lexi says it's what they used to call a *trappers' hut*. From early in the last century, when the Raincoast was just wilderness. The first settlers were animal trappers and fur traders who built these huts out in the woods. The horns are actually chimneys made from cans and tin drums welded together, with smaller cans on top. In the historical photo she dug up, they do kind of look like horns, thinning almost to points at the top.

So now we're trying to find out if any still exist. There must be one. That's where Leo died.

"Jane?"

I snap back to see Dr. Simon staring at me.

"What?"

"Do you have any questions?" he asks.

I look over at my brain on the screen, the nail shining darkly.

"No. Let's just do it."

35

"Are you afraid?" my psychiatrist asks.

I stare back at Dr. Iris.

"Afraid of what?"

My life has turned into a multiple choice of horrors. Pick one.

"You're going in for major surgery," she says.

"Well, yeah, that's scary stuff. But I kind of want to get it over with. Can't keep walking around like a ticking time bomb. Then I think, what if something goes wrong and when I wake up—*if* I wake up—I'm not me anymore?"

"There's always some risk involved, but these operations are very precise. Neurosurgeons take every precaution. You'll be in good hands."

Easy for her to say. She's not having her skull sawed open.

"But it just takes one wrong twitch of the surgeon's fingers and I'll be a drooling vegetable. What if he sneezes when he's cutting?"

"It might be best to focus on what you can control," she tells me. "Like lowering your stress level."

Right. I can't even control my own body. The bandage on my wrist is showing a little, so I tug on my sleeve to hide it.

I'm sick of being stared at—here, in class, across the dinner table. I get up and walk around the room, avoiding her eyes.

"How are your parents handling it?" she asks.

I pass by the potted palm tree in the corner, brushing my fingers over its flat leaves. They make a dry whisper.

"My mom's a nervous wreck. Takes my temperature ten times a day. She's read enough about brain surgery to do it herself."

After my ghost cornered me in the basement yesterday, I slept with Mom again. I haven't shared her bed so much since I was little. She likes having me close right now, so she didn't ask why.

"And your father? How is he dealing with it?"

I shrug. "He's a cop. A natural fixer. And what's hurting me, he can't fix. So I guess it's eating away at him."

There's an aquarium set against the wall. I bend to gaze at the crazy-colored tropical fish. Reminds me of the terrarium I saw in Leo's room—with the frogs he kept—in those flashes of memory he shared with me when I died. He was collecting tadpoles from a pond when he was taken.

"You know they identified the remains uncovered by that landslide? Those bones I saw. The murdered kid. He's got a name now."

"Yes, I saw on the news. How are you coping with all that?"

I'm about to say, *Badly.* But then I get an idea. Maybe Doc Iris can help me with my shadow-ghost problem.

"I'm trying to get a grip on it." I sit down again. "How could anyone do that to a kid? They'd have to be a psycho, right? I mean, do you think these child-killers are just born that way? All twisted. Or does something happen to make them into monsters?"

I'm not really asking about Leo's killer, but about Leo himself. Because he's my monster. Maybe my doctor can analyze him, help me figure him out.

"Well, in cases like this, where the victim was so young, you'll usually find that the killers were victims themselves when they were children."

"Victims of what?"

"Violence. Usually sexual abuse. It's not uncommon for the abused to become the abuser."

Is that it? Was my ghost so warped by what happened in that black house that he turned into a monster himself?

"Have you dealt with any guys who were abused like that?" I ask.

"Yes, I've counseled some."

"What are they like? I mean, what kind of damage does it do to them?"

"It can be emotionally crippling. They're afflicted with a deep sense of shame and are left feeling worthless. They feel as if they're marked by what was done to them, that nobody could ever love them again. Some isolate themselves, not wanting their families to see them after."

"And some get violent?"

She nods. "But you need to focus on yourself right now, Jane. You look exhausted."

I sigh. "Yeah. I'm beat."

"Get some rest. Forget everything else. Give yourself a mental vacation."

"Sounds good to me."

Take a vacation from my life. Go somewhere far away. And leave my ghost behind.

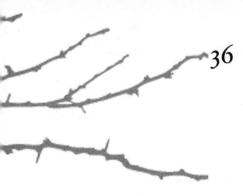

36

I wake up in the dark with the wind in my face. Rain chilling my skin.

My scream comes out as a ragged gasp.

What? Where am I?

Shaking my head, I try to clear it.

Must have been sleepwalking. But how did I get out of the house without setting off the alarm?

I hold up my hand, checking for my ring. It's gone. I know I wore it to bed. Maybe I took it off in my sleep. Do they even know I'm gone? Mom and Dad will be frantic.

The moon shines a cool blue light down on me through a gap in the clouds. Where am I? Out in the open.

My feet are like ice. Looking down at them—

I nearly stumble forward. But I stop myself in time, arms out to keep my balance.

My toes are curled over the edge of nothing. The ground ends in a sharp drop. I hear the waves breaking down below, invisible in the dark.

An updraft whips my hair around, smelling of salt

water and seaweed. I fight the shiver in my legs that could tip me over the cliff.

Don't panic!

Gravity sucks at my knees, trying to get them to fold. If I lean just the slightest bit . . .

Don't even twitch!

But my legs shake. Ready to give out.

I stumble back, away from the cliff, and fall hard on the rocks.

My T-shirt and sweatpants are soaked.

Leaning up on my elbows, I try to figure where I am. Off to my right, down a steep slope, I can see the lights of Edgewood.

This must be Lookout Hill. They call it that for the view, and because if you don't look out you'll be taking a high dive onto the broken reefs.

If I hadn't woken up just now—what then? Would they be fishing me out of the surf tomorrow?

Is this my shadow trying to kill me again? Two more days till they take the nail out. If I can just make it till then.

The wind freezes through my wet clothes.

Get moving. Get up!

Rolling onto my knees, I'm about to push myself to my feet when I see it. I'm not alone.

He's standing by the drop in front of me. Wearing his hooded sweatshirt and jeans. Watching, amber eyes glowing.

I don't move. Don't breathe.

So close, his voice whispers in my head. *You come right up to the edge. But you always pull back.*

I see now that he's not standing on the cliff at all, but a few yards past the cutoff. Nothing beneath him but air.

Go! Run! But my legs are so shivery I can't trust them to hold me up.

Come with me.

He reaches his hand out.

I shake my head.

His hand falls back to his side.

Don't make me hurt you.

He sounds almost sad.

"No!" I yell. "You're not—not going to hurt me anymore! They're cutting this thing out of my head. And when it's gone, you'll be gone too. Back to sleep. Back where you came from."

You can't get rid of me. I'm part of you.

"You're nothing to me! Nothing!"

He shuts his eyes for a moment, snuffing their fire.

But you're everything to me. His voice quiets to a hush, like he's telling a secret. *Since we first met.*

"We never met!" I shout. "You went missing before I was even born."

We met before.

"Before what?"

His eyes open, flaring bright.

Before your first breath.

A cold deeper than the night wind sinks into me.

When you were born dead. And your soul drifted away. I found you, lost in the dark. Lost like me.

I don't want to hear this.

Your soul was so new and bright. Like a firefly. I kept you close, kept you safe. And you were mine.

The breath shudders out of me, clouding in the frigid air.

But they took you from me.

I force myself to ask. "They?"

The doctors. They made your newborn heart beat when it wasn't meant to.

I'm shivering all over.

But I never let go.

He was always there? Before my first breath?

"But why? Why did you have to hurt me all those times?"

You were meant for me. Nobody else.

I squeeze my eyes shut to break away from his gaze. When I open them again I scramble backward on the slick rocks, getting my feet under me.

And I run. Frantic and stumbling in the rainy dark.

You're mine.

His voice follows as I rush downhill. Everywhere I look I see yellow afterimages of his eyes, flames burning in the night.

Mine.

I keep going, fast as I can.

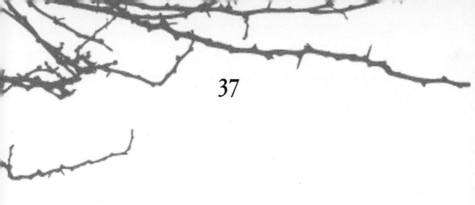

37

This must be what going crazy feels like. When all your delusions start making sense. And I guess the worst thing about being nuts is how alone you are, when you're the only one hearing the voices or seeing the ghosts.

If I didn't have Lexi to prove I'm not nuts, I'd be so lost.

When I got back from Lookout Hill late last night I was surprised all the lights in the house weren't blazing, that Mom wasn't on red alert. But the place was dark and sleeping still. Nobody even knew I was gone. I managed to slip inside and up to my room, where I found my ring on the floor beside my bed. Mom and Dad think they don't have to check up on me at night now as long as the alarm doesn't go off.

I was so exhausted and cold from the long run home that it was a struggle just to get out of my wet clothes and into some dry ones. Then I collapsed in bed.

In the morning, I felt almost human again. But still shaky. The one thing keeping me from totally falling apart is knowing I only have two more days till the operation.

It's near noon on Saturday. The house is quiet. By now Mom will be down at the Blushing Rose.

I find a note from her stuck on the doorknob of my room: *Don't forget your pills.*

I take a long hot shower to thaw out.

I'm still in shock from what Leo told me last night. It's like the whole history of my life just got rewritten.

He's always been there with me—every breath, every heartbeat—hiding in my shadow.

I let the heat of the shower sink into me, breathing the steam and losing myself for a while in the mist.

Drying off, I check my computer and find half a dozen new messages from Lexi this morning. But none of them urgent. So I click on her email from two days ago instead. The one where she showed me the trappers' hut.

Like in the rough sketch my shadow made me draw, the horns stick up from opposite ends of the roof. The reason it has those two chimneys is that one was for the living space, and the other was for the room where the trappers butchered and smoked their meat.

While I've been busy with doctors and tests, Lexi has been searching online archives, trying to find out if any of these huts are still standing.

I've got to tell her about last night. But I need to wake all the way up first and get something to eat. I'm starving.

Downstairs I find Dad slouched and snoring on the couch, his mouth hanging open. He's still in uniform from the night shift.

I watch him for a minute, wanting to wake him up and

tell him what's really going on. When I was growing up, he always made me feel safe. But he can't save me from something he could never even believe in.

Spread out on the coffee table in front of him are heaps of files. Sneaking a peek, I see that they're all about Leo Gage. Nearly twenty years of investigating this case adds up to a mountain of paperwork.

I quietly shuffle through a small stack, finding interviews with Gage's family, friends, classmates, teachers and neighbors.

The officers ask the same questions again and again: When did you see Leo last? Any problems at home, at school? Had he made any new friends lately? Gotten in any fights? Has he ever run away?

Another stack has more interviews, but these have cover sheets with mug shots. Registered sex offenders. Dad says it's standard procedure to check out the local sickos when any kid goes missing. I do a quick flip through their shots. None look familiar.

Buried under all this paperwork I find a thick file with another boy's MISSING poster attached to the cover. Christopher Ford. Twelve years old. Inside, I find a copy of his autopsy report. He's not missing anymore.

Dad lets out a loud snort, waking himself up. He looks over, blinking me into focus.

"Hi, Boo."

"Hi, Bulldog. You've got a little drool on your chin there."

He swipes it away with his sleeve. "What're you snooping at?"

I show him the kid's photo. "Who's he?"

He squints at it, sighing. "Another dead boy."

"So is he connected somehow to the Leo Gage case?"

Dad stretches with a groan. "Nothing like waking up to an interrogation. We don't know if there's a connection. He was missing for three years before his body turned up. Buried in the forest."

"But it says here he was found way over in Tumbler Ridge. That's a long way from Edgewood."

"Two hundred and twenty miles."

"So is there anything that links the two deaths?"

He rubs the sleep out of his eyes. "Not yet. But the profiler experts see a possible pattern. The victimology is too similar to ignore."

"What's that mean?"

He reaches over and takes the file from me, slipping it back in the envelope. "You don't need to hear any of this."

"Sure I do. I was there when you found the kid's bones. Really, I need to know."

Dad scratches his fingers through his gray hair. "Well, the profiles of the victims are very close. Both were twelve or thirteen, white, taken from rural towns along the coast and found buried in heavily wooded areas. And the autopsies show the probable cause of death is the same: fractured skull."

"So what are you saying? You're looking for some kind of serial killer?"

"Who knows? It's a possibility. A theory. But two hundred or so miles is a lot of geography between the burial sites. Serials usually like to cluster them closer together."

"Why do they do that?" I ask.

"So they can go back and . . . visit them. Relive it all."

Dad starts stacking the files. I notice a large yellow envelope with MCD in big black letters.

I point it out. "What's in that one? MCD?"

"Those are bulletins from the Missing Children's Database. Open cases of missing kids from across the province who fit the same basic profile."

"More victims?"

"No. Hope not. Most missing kids turn up as runaways or parental abductions. Leave this stuff to me, Boo. It's my job."

Dad heads for the kitchen, and I follow. There's a note stuck to the handle of the fridge door.

"'Make sure she takes her pills'," he reads.

"I know. I know."

"Hey, don't let your mother know we've been talking about this stuff. You're supposed to be resting. No stress. No drama."

Right. Talk to my ghost.

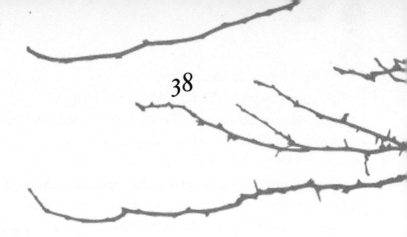

38

I try to catch my breath. I've been talking nonstop for the past ten minutes, telling Lexi everything about last night on the cliff. Pacing around her room, ranting and raving till I run out of air.

I sit down on the desk chair, breathless but feeling a little better. Now that I've shared the madness, I don't seem so alone in it.

"Wow," Lexi says. "Haunted from the start. You never had a chance."

I just shake my head. Damn, is that really the story of my life?

Above her desk, I see she's been expanding her "wall of death." Besides the afterlife images with the otherworldly light, spirits and souls in flight, the rest of the space is dedicated to my ghost. A collage of pictures and articles, from Leo Gage's original MISSING poster to the old newspaper stories to the flood of new coverage.

The initial searches led nowhere. They dredged nearby ponds, scoured the coastline, ran down hundreds of tips.

But it was like he just stepped out of the world that day. Into nothing.

"The way he talked about how we met. You know, how our souls were both lost in the dark? It sounded a lot like the Divide."

That place of never-ending night separating the living world from the light.

I've checked out all the websites about near-death experiences, with stories brought back by Second Chancers like me. I've been trying to figure out why some souls get trapped in that void and become Grim Enders. Why won't they go to the light?

I found out that the light *feels* different to some people. For most, like me, it was this perfect healing sunshine, taking away all my pain and fears, giving me a deep sense of peace.

But for some it burns. In these rare cases the light hurts so much they pull back from it. Those who have experienced this pain describe it as feeling like their soul was set on fire.

Why does it burn them? They say the light makes you truly see yourself. Makes you face all your fears, your guilt and shame, the bad you've done, and the damage that's been done to you. The light brings out your deepest darkness. Then burns it away in a flash.

But when the dark goes so deep in you that's it's taken over—if you can't let go or can't face it—then the moment of pain from the fire doesn't end. And your soul is left in agony.

Those who can't give up their darkness are doomed. Scared of the light, they lose themselves in the Divide.

"So Leo tried to kill you," Lexi says. "To take you back. All because he thinks you belong together? Belong to him? That's a twisted kind of love."

"It was never about love." I pick at the bandage on my wrist. "He wants to *own* me. I'm all he's got, and he won't share."

"We have to do something to keep you safe till surgery." Lexi leans on the desk next to me. "There's no way you're sleeping alone anymore. I'm going to crash at your place till your operation."

"Be my bodyguard?"

"Hell, yeah. You need guarding."

What would I do without my Creep Sister?

"Then you're hired. I'll pay you in pizza." Trying out a small smile, I glance at the ghost wall beside us. "All this work. You've been busy."

"You know me. Maniac insomniac. Which makes me a perfect night watchman." Lexi grabs her mug off the desk. "I need caffeine to keep up with this weirdness. You want some coffee?"

"Sure. But decaf."

While she heads downstairs, I let my eyes wander over the wall. Leo's MISSING poster shows him smiling. What changed him? Was he warped by the Divide, the total isolation and loneliness? Or was it what happened to him in that house of horrors he drew for me?

Lexi's been emailing me these bits and pieces. When I see it all together, there are so many details that I can't tell what might be important and what's nothing. It's been barely two weeks since the landslide uncovered those bones. But it feels way longer, like it's been January forever.

I spot that famous photo of me on the wall, the awful image taken after the landslide unearthed the skull. I'm standing behind Dad. The skull seems to glow in the glare of the flashlight.

Near that picture are the drawings I made under my shadow's influence. Those half-torn pages showing the bird and the house stained with my blood.

Leaning back in the chair, I try to force all this info into meaning something. Give me some answers. But the wall keeps its secrets.

One photo catches my eye. Dad's in it. The shot was taken at the press conference to announce the task force assigned to the case, with a row of law enforcement officials standing behind Constable Granger at the podium. They've brought in the top federal cops, police from neighboring counties, the coast guard, profilers and all kinds of forensics experts.

Dad's gray hair looks snowier than usual. When did he get so old? How much of that is because of me?

There are other news photos of the crime lab team searching for evidence in the landslide.

The forest trails near the burial site were blocked off. They fall within the boundaries of Raincoast National Park. A picture shows some official in a green uniform setting up a wooden barrier that says TRAIL CLOSED NO ENTRY ALLOWED.

He seems familiar somehow, the man in green. Have I seen him in town?

Getting up, I lean over the desk for a closer look.

It's bugging me. Where do I know him from?

Something about him gives me the creeps. He's tall, really skinny and bald.

Then an image flashes behind my eyes.

For a split second it's like I'm somewhere else, seeing another place as clearly as the room around me. I see—

A bald, spidery thin man, standing by a pond in the woods. Grinning, with cold dark eyes. There's a black bird riding on his shoulder, a crow. The man reaches out a bony hand. And I know his touch will mean something worse than death.

Snapping back to Lexi's room, I feel like the breath's been sucked out of me.

No way! That can't be him—the bald man from my vision. The one who got Leo.

I rip the picture off the wall, searching the caption. He's identified as Park Ranger Garrett Starks.

I can't believe it. But there he is.

I jump when the door creaks open behind me, and Lexi walks in holding two mugs. She stops when she sees the shock on my face.

"What's wrong?"

I remember to breathe again.

"Look at this." I hold up the picture. "It's him. Right there."

She comes over. "Who's that?"

"He's the killer."

39

"This is a bad idea," Lexi tells me.

"Maybe. But I have to see it with my own eyes. See *him*. So I can be sure."

It's late afternoon on this misty Saturday, a couple of hours after I discovered that photo of the ranger. We're sitting in her car, just outside of town, in the parking lot of the Raincoast National Park ranger station.

"Okay," she says. "Just as long as he doesn't see *you*."

We checked the place out online. Besides overseeing park service operations, they sell camping and fishing permits, and there's a gift shop with tourist stuff.

"That's why I'm undercover." I try and joke, but my heart's going a mile a minute, and I can feel cold sweat running down my back.

My undercover look has me wearing a pair of sunglasses and a black slicker, with my hair pulled back in a ponytail, hidden beneath a baseball cap.

Lexi's shaking her head. "He's probably following the media coverage of the case. What if he's seen that photo with you and your dad at the landslide?"

"Don't worry. My own mother wouldn't recognize me in this getup."

"You sure about this?"

"Positive."

"Okay." She slips on her own shades. "It looks like a bunch of tourists are in there now. Let's do this while there's a crowd. And make it quick. In and out."

We cross the parking lot.

The station is a log-built lodge next to the entrance road to the park. Inside we find the gift shop and pretend to check out the postcards. Sitting behind the register, a nerdy guy is playing a game on his phone.

Lexi nods toward a hallway that leads deeper into the lodge. We follow it to the main area.

I spot a woman in a green ranger uniform handing out brochures to an old couple. There's a TV playing a fishing program. And behind a long counter another ranger is unfolding a large map for a group of tourists.

I stop dead in my tracks. It's *him*.

Garrett Starks. Tall and gaunt, his bald head pale. Laying down the map, he points something out with a bony finger.

I flash back to my vision of that same spidery hand reaching for Leo, to take him away.

Something touches my elbow, making me flinch.

"Let's go," Lexi whispers in my ear. "Now."

Turning to leave, I catch him looking my way. But it's just a quick glance, not stopping on me.

Then I'm rushing down the hall, out into the parking

lot. Desperate to get away and escape the reach of those hands.

Me and Lexi start our own task force, headquartered in my bedroom. She's sleeping over, and brought her laptop with all the news files and photos she's collected about the case.

I'm still shaken up after seeing him in the flesh. It was bad enough having that image of him in my head from the borrowed memory of my ghost. Spotting him in the real world, with my own eyes, was terrifying. But I had to be sure.

While Lexi works at my desk, I sit on my bed with my computer, searching for info on Garrett Starks.

So far what we've got on Starks is sketchy. The National Parks Service site gave a basic bio. He's thirty-eight years old, been a ranger for eighteen. Grew up down the coast in Long Beach—just outside Ferny, Leo's hometown. Starks would have been twenty when Leo Gage went missing. There's a picture showing the man in his green uniform, standing in front of the Raincoast National Park ranger station. He's grinning, but it's a cold smile that doesn't reach the eyes.

Lexi dug up a few minor mentions of him in the local papers. Official stuff, like giving out Parks Service warnings during forest fire season, reporting bear and wolf sightings, talking about vanishing frog populations and the decreasing salmon runs.

While Lexi was finding that stuff, I used Dad's

computer in his home office to sneak a peek into the Edgewood Police Department's database. Not the first time I've gone snooping. There's no hacking required because I've seen him log in before, so I know his password is programmed into one of the function keys.

Starks's criminal background check turned up clean. No history of any charges or arrests. Which just means he's a real pro, knows how to hide what he is.

It's after midnight and my vision's going fuzzy from staring at the screen so long. Lexi's still bright-eyed.

"You gotta see this," she says.

I get up from the bed, stretching. "Whatcha got?"

"It's a website for kids, linked up with the National Parks site. Looks like Garrett Starks runs it. He calls himself Ranger G."

I pull up a chair.

"See where it says you can book field trips to the station?" Lexi points. "That's a perfect way to shop for fresh victims. He even does school visits."

"What's that there?" I point to a video link that says *Come See Ranger G and the Amazing Blackjack*. "Click on it."

The picture that comes up stops me cold. Starks is in uniform, smiling, his dark eyes shining. A bird is perched on his outstretched hand. A big black crow.

"Is that the bird you saw?" Lexi asks.

"That's it. Run the video."

She clicks and they come to life.

"Meet Blackjack the crow," Starks says, his cheerful voice making me cringe. "His bird brain may be only the size of a grape, but he can do some amazing tricks."

Starks holds his left hand out with the crow balancing on his index finger. Then he makes his other hand into a pretend gun.

"This is a stickup," he tells Blackjack. "Get your wings in the air."

The crow stretches its wings out. Starks points his finger-gun and makes like he's pulling the trigger.

"Bang!"

Blackjack falls backward with a screaming squawk, still clinging to Starks's index finger, and ends up hanging from it upside down. "Now you're dead," Starks says. Then he makes a flipping motion with his left hand and the crow flaps upright, back on top of the ranger's hand again. "And now you're not."

The image freezes there with Starks and Blackjack staring at each other. A message pops up on the screen: *Click here for more tricks.*

"He uses that bird," Lexi says, "to lure the kids in. That's classic abductor strategy. You know, the whole 'Can you help me find my puppy?' or 'You want to pet the bunny?' kind of thing."

I feel disgusted, seeing him in action, hearing the sound of his voice. "That makes me nauseous."

"What do we do now?" she asks. "I mean, you can't actually tell anyone how you know he's the killer. Maybe if they search his stuff they'll find something. These psychos like to keep souvenirs, don't they?"

"You can't get a search warrant without a solid reason. Bad dreams and near-death visions don't count."

"So what, then?" Lexi says.

"Don't know." I shake my head. "But if we could find that trappers' hut, we might have something. That's where it all happened, where Leo died. Any luck tracking one of those down?"

"I actually did find a couple of them online, but they don't look promising." Lexi clears the image of Starks off the screen and brings up a photo. A sunny shot of a house with horns, looking bright and well kept. "This one was turned into a pioneer tourist place decades ago, with a little gift shop and everything. Not exactly a house of horrors." A new picture pops up. "Here's the other hut. Or what's left of it." This one's falling apart, with a collapsed roof and the twin "horn" chimneys tilted over. The hut is overgrown with vegetation; it looks like the forest is reclaiming its turf. "It's obviously been in ruins for a long, long time."

I let out a deep sigh. "Maybe we could check with the historical society over at town hall. They keep track of landmarks and old stuff, right?"

"Worth a try."

After taking a break and raiding the kitchen, we settle in with corn chips and popcorn to watch the movie Lexi made by editing all the bits and pieces of TV coverage together, telling the tragic story of Leo Gage. From home movies of his childhood through his disappearance, the long investigation and the discovery of his remains.

This is how Lexi makes sense of things, by turning them into movies. The same way she's always editing and reediting all the old home movies her father shot, splicing them together so many different ways, trying to find where and why everything broke down. She's still working on the final cut of that.

We come to some footage from a news show that covers cold cases. I nibble popcorn and try to focus, looking for any small hint or clue that might help. But I'm so burned out. Maybe Lexi can go sleepless, but I'm ready to crash.

"Lexi, what do you say we—"

My voice dies, and I go stiff as something snakes up my spine.

"What's wrong?" Lexi says.

I turn to look behind me. Nothing. But I know this feeling.

"He's here."

"You sure?"

I nod, breathing faster now. Lexi grabs my hands.

"Hey, Jane. Look at me. I'm not going to let anything happen to you." I focus on her eyes, desperate to believe her. "I've got an idea. Come with me."

She pulls me up and takes me over to my dresser, letting go so she can open the drawers.

"Here, put these on."

"What?" I stare at the pair of thick socks she's holding out. "Why?"

"On your hands. Slip them on. Just do it!"

I give up asking why and go with it. The long winter socks reach nearly to my elbows.

"Good," she says. "Now, do you have any rubber bands, or something?"

"Um, I guess. Check the desk."

Lexi goes through the top drawer. "Hey, even better." She pulls out a roll of duct tape.

I can see where she's headed now. "You gotta be kidding me."

But she isn't. I hold out my arms to her.

"Okay. Do it."

Two minutes later I'm back in the chair, feeling a little calmer. The socks are taped up to my skin, just below the elbows. Can't hurt myself now. Or take off my ring. Can't do anything.

"What's next?" I ask. "A straitjacket?"

She tries to smile. "He still here?"

I nod. His touch is writhing between my shoulder blades.

The movie keeps playing, with the sound on low.

"How about if we watch something else?" she says. "To distract you, maybe."

I nod, and she reaches over to kill the video.

On the screen, Leo's mother is being interviewed. Just as she starts talking, a little jolt runs through me, making me gasp.

"You okay?" Lexi asks.

The mother's voice hits me with a wave of sadness. A deep aching. A hurt that doesn't belong to me, coming from my ghost. I can sense Leo pulling back from me.

"Wait!" I stop Lexi from ending the movie.

"Why? What's going on?"

I get an idea. "Turn up the volume."

She does, and we can hear the mother's voice clearly, breaking into sobs now as she talks about her lost son.

My trembling melts away.

"He can't take it. Seeing her. Hearing her."

As his mother's crying fills the room, I feel him leaving. Taking the pain with him. The shared emotions fade to nothing.

"He's gone. That was too much for him."

"Hang in there," Lexi says, rubbing my back, and the warmth of her hand wipes away the leftover shivers.

We let the footage run for a while longer, till I'm sure he'll stay gone.

After that Lexi plays some cartoons, desperately trying to lighten the mood.

Later, when I'm falling off my chair, exhausted, Lexi tells me to go to bed.

"I'm here," she says. "Don't worry. You're safe."

So I get under the sheets, dozing off with socks on my hands and Lexi watching over me.

40

This is my last night. Surgery tomorrow.

Lexi's taking her bodyguarding seriously, not letting me out of her sight, and ready to step in if my ghost tries to make me hurt myself. I'm wearing my magic ring for extra tracking protection. My hands are unbound and sock-free for now.

Last night while I was sleeping, Lexi was busy reworking the old TV clips of Leo's mother into a five-minute segment we can use to scare him off if he comes back.

"That's brilliant," I told her as she peeled the duct tape off my arms this morning.

"I know. Genius never sleeps."

We spent my last day out around town. The rain held off, and we went over to Sunset Beach, watching the windsurfers in their wetsuits ride the frigid waves. Seeing Lexi film them gave me an idea.

I asked to borrow her camera and a spare disc.

"So I can record a message for my mom and dad. Just in case something goes wrong. You know, in the surgery."

"Nothing's going to go wrong, Jane."

"They'll be digging in my brain. I could end up a vegetable."

"Shut up."

"I'm just saying—"

"Yeah, and I'm just saying quit it. You're gonna be fine."

So I shut up. She's scared too, and covering it up with denial. She wanted to do the filming for me—Lexi the director—but I said I needed to do it alone.

"It'll be hard enough without an audience."

Lexi gave me some space, wandering off down the beach.

I sat down on a log in the sand, with the wind blowing my hair around and the sound of surf in the background.

Making the message was really hard. I thought I could do it in one take, but then I started choking up and tearing up, with my voice breaking and my nose running—a total mess. So I kept having to go back and tape over.

I ended up recording a worst-case-scenario *goodbye* kind of thing for Mom and Dad. That was tough stuff. Hope they never have to see it.

I gave the disc to Lexi for safekeeping. For just in case.

Anyway, right now it's getting late. We're back in my room, with the music on and a double feature of our favorite comedies ready to roll on my computer. I'm under orders from Mom and Lexi to rest and relax.

Really, there's nothing more I can do about Leo and Starks right now. Me and Lexi can figure out our next move when I'm better. When my ghost problem is hopefully put back to sleep.

Standing in front of the full-length mirror on my closet door, I'm checking out how I'm going to look after the operation.

I hate my frizzy hair, which never does what I want. But I'm going to miss it. Tomorrow it's all coming off. And I just know *bald* ain't gonna be a good look for me.

Lexi watches as I squeeze my head into one of Mom's tight swimming caps, tucking my hair out of sight.

"That's scary," I say.

"It's not so bad," Lexi lies.

With nothing to soften my face, my big eyes look huge. I mean, I already look like somebody just set off a firecracker next to me, but now they're cartoon big. And my hair usually keeps these satellite-dish ears hidden.

"I'm going to look like an alien."

"So we'll go shopping for wigs. Get you a blond Afro, maybe. Or some dreadlocks."

"I can't get into the wig thing. I'd feel like there was a furry animal sitting on top of my head."

"How about a beret, then? Or a cowboy hat?" Lexi says, but I shake my head. "I know, a sombrero?"

I roll my eyes, pulling the cap off to free my mane again.

Lexi grabs another piece of pizza from the box on my desk. Triple cheese. Smells good, but I'm not supposed to eat anything this close to surgery. Not real hungry anyway.

As she stuffs her face, Lexi picks up one of my romance novels. *Stormheart*. The cover shows the pirate queen Felicia on the deck of her ship, with a sword in her hand and a gleam of lust in her eyes. At the tip of her blade stands her enemy and future lover, Damon.

Lexi flips it open and reads, "'Felicia's auburn hair cascaded over her dewy bosom.'"

I grab it away.

"Dewy," Lexi snorts. "Seriously, you should write one of those. You could do better than that."

I shake my head. "I've tried. But me writing about romance is like . . . like a blind girl describing colors she's never seen."

Lexi swallows a mouthful of pizza. "Don't get all sad and *dewy*-eyed on me. You ready for a movie?"

I put *Stormheart* in my closet love library. "Go ahead and cue one up. I'll be right back."

I'm out in the hall when I realize she's following me.

"I'm just going to the bathroom, Lexi. That's kind of a solo act."

"Okay. But let me check it out first. Make sure there's nothing potentially dangerous."

I can hear Mom downstairs in the kitchen, so I lower my voice.

"What am I going to do, scrub myself to death?"

"You never know. Your shadow's pretty sneaky. Right now you really are your own worst enemy."

Can't argue with that. "I guess you're right. After you, then."

She leads the way and does a quick check of the medicine cabinet and the cupboard under the sink, confiscating scissors and the hair dryer.

"What, am I going to blow-dry my brains out?"

"Electrocution. You could fill up the tub and toss it in. Or stand in the toilet with it plugged in and drop it."

"I think my craziness is rubbing off on you."

"Okay. It's clear now." She's like my very own secret service agent making sure the room is safe before I go in.

I close the door behind me and look at myself in the mirror.

Running my fingers through my hair, I unsnarl some knots, saying a silent goodbye to it all. My thumb finds the little dent where the nail entered, and the bumps left behind when they took out the stitches. It's still just a tiny bit tender as I touch it, like the memory of a bee sting. The patch of scalp they shaved there is growing some hair again. I rub at the purple scar visible under that new fuzz, like I can erase it somehow.

After I pee, I'm washing my hands when I feel a rush of dizziness. As I brace myself on the sink, my reflection in the mirror goes blurry. What's this? My eyes tearing up? I try to blink it away.

But no. It's not tears messing with my focus.

The faucet's still running. I want to splash some cold water on my face, but I feel stuck.

Hard to think. My head's filled with fog. This feels wrong.

I try to call out, but can't make a sound. I'm losing control.

I see everything from a distance, like it's happening to somebody else. I can make out a shadowy blur; then my hands are moving, fingers working. And I hear the metal clink of something falling in the sink.

My ring.

Then I'm climbing. Up on top of the toilet. Reaching out and opening the small window above it. Pulling myself up and squeezing through.

I slip out onto the slope of the roof below the window. Into the cold and the wind. Crawling on wet shingles, over to the edge.

Is he going to make me jump? Throw myself off?

But my hands grip the rain gutter at the corner of the roof. I swing over the edge, climb down the metal pipe and fall the last few feet to the grass.

The fog in my head is so thick I can't see a thing. He's smothering my mind, knocking me out.

But I can feel myself standing up. My legs start moving, carrying me away.

Where are you taking me? I try to ask.

I'm picking up speed. Faster. It's like running with my eyes shut.

Racing blind.

But where?

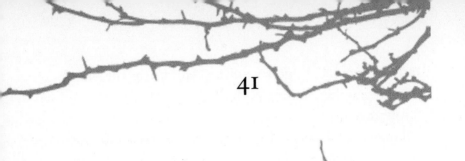

41

I snap awake standing in total blackness.

My lungs are burning, my legs aching. How long have I been running? How far?

Reaching out, I hit something rough and pull back. But it's just tree bark. I can barely see my own hand in front of me, only a pale smudge.

My heart is thudding. All I hear is rain dripping from branches. Feeling around, I find thick trunks surrounding me and breathe in the smell of wet pine.

I try to make my way through the bodies of the trees. How lost am I now? Where—

A scream rips through the night, freezing me up.

No. Not a scream. More like . . . a screech. Like a bird up in the branches above me.

Get a grip, Jane! Don't lose it.

My eyes are adjusting to the blackness. I catch a faint light through the trees and follow it. I'm stumbling along in my torn wet socks, my feet so sore it feels like I've just run a marathon.

The stupid bird comes with me, making me flinch every time it calls out.

Everybody must be going crazy right now with me disappearing. If I can just make it to a phone somewhere, or even a road so I can figure out where I am.

Please! I just want to go home.

In my T-shirt and pajama bottoms, I hug myself against the cold and head for that glow.

The trees are thinning out. I stop at the edge of a clearing. The light's coming from a small house. The windows are boarded up, but a glow leaks out through the cracks.

I wait and watch a minute, but nothing's moving. No signs of life. I really don't like this.

Now that my eyes are used to the dark, I notice something strange about that house. And I go stiff.

It has horns!

A trappers' hut.

I know where I am.

Get out of here! Go!

The bird screeches down at me again. Can't see it, but I know what it must be. A crow.

Blackjack.

Get out! Now!

Turning away, I'm hit by a blinding light. My hands fly up to shield my eyes.

"You lost?" asks a low voice, male.

A flashlight is aimed right in my eyes. Can't see past its glare. I only get an impression of the man's height, looming over me.

I back up into a tree trunk. It's him!

Say something. "Y-yeah. Lost."

"Where were you headed?"

"I was . . . just meeting up with my friend. Must have turned down the wrong road."

A moment of silence goes by.

"Do I know you?" he asks.

"No. I—I mean, I don't think so."

"I've seen you somewhere. I never forget a face."

"I really—really have to go. My friend's waiting."

I take a step away, but he moves with me.

"Hey, I know. You're that cop's daughter. Aren't you? I saw your picture in the paper, and on the news."

Damn! I can't deny it or he'll know something's up.

"Yeah."

"Right. Saw you on the news. You were there at the landslide, when they spotted the dead boy's bones."

"Yeah." I step back and nearly trip over some roots. "Anyway, I should be going."

"What are you doing way out here? In the middle of nowhere?" He doesn't sound threatening, but almost friendly, like he's making small talk.

"Just took a wrong turn."

I start walking along the edge of the clearing, my hands out to feel my way past the trees.

"Lost, eh?" He follows along. "Why don't you come inside? You can call your father."

If I go in there I'll probably never make it out again.

"No. Thanks."

He keeps the light on me. Can't see a thing. Which way to run.

"I can't let you go like this. In the dark and the rain."

"I'll be okay."

A few seconds pass with only my shaky breathing and racing heartbeat loud in my ears.

"You know, like I was saying, I've got a real memory for faces. Did you happen to be out at the ranger's station yesterday?"

My heart squeezes tight. "No."

"You sure?"

"Y-yeah. Must have been somebody else." My voice is breaking up.

"No, I don't think so." His voice is still calm and friendly. "You been following me?"

"No. No, of course not."

Can I outrun him? Lose him in the trees?

"This place is way too far from anything for any kind of *wrong turn*. And you didn't come down the wrong road, because there are no roads out here."

I just shake my head. Go! Now!

"Funny thing," he says. "You being there at the landslide when those bones showed up, then you show up at the station. And now you're sneaking around here in the middle of the night, spying on the place." He puts his hand on my shoulder. "I don't think you're lost."

His grip on me tightens. He turns the flashlight off, and the night seems darker than ever.

"Please, I—"

Then something else flares to life in his hand, with a crackling blue light. A jagged electric flash.

Stun gun!

I try to pull away.

He hits me in the ribs with it. The shock rips through me like lightning. I go rigid. Muscles clenched tight.

Shaking wildly, I drop to my knees.

Falling, my head hits the ground hard. I lie limp.

But it feels like I'm still falling.

Down and

down and

down.

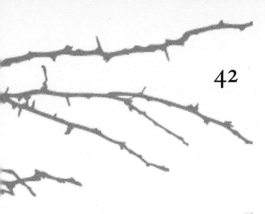

42

I wake up surrounded by blue light.

What is this? Where am I?

I ache all over, my head throbbing with my heartbeat.

I'm lying on my back with my shoulders pressed up against hard surfaces. Squeezed in tight. Trying to get my eyes to focus, I make out another flat surface right above, closing me in.

A coffin?

No. I'm not thinking straight. My head's messed up.

Can't be. Must be dreaming.

With that blue glow it seems more like a drawer. In a morgue!

No. Stop it! I shake my head, making it pound even harder. How did I get here? Where's here? And what hit me? The last thing I remember—

The ranger! Catching me. The electric flash of the stun gun. The shock burning through me. I fell and kept on falling. Then—here.

In the morgue? A coffin?

My nightmares are coming true.

No. No. No.

Think! I blink my eyes into focus. Where's that light coming from?

Reaching up, I'm able to extend my arm before my fingers touch what feels like stone above. It's stone all around, the walls wedging me in.

With an effort I turn on my side and get to my knees. I stay hunched over, no room to sit up. I'm shaking real bad, and breathing fast.

There's a strong chemical smell in the air. Like ammonia or some kind of cleaner.

Now I see what's making that blue light. It's a long fluorescent tube on the wall. In the glow I can make out the rest of this cramped space. From where I'm crouched at one end, it's about eight feet to the other end, where there's a pile of blankets heaped up.

This is like some kind of jail cell. A cage made of concrete. What's going on?

Sorry.

I stiffen up at the voice in my head. Leo. I feel that familiar shiver. He's here with me.

"You did this! You brought me here."

I didn't want to do it like this.

"Get out of my head."

I tried to make it quick. And painless. But you always fought it.

Scanning this cell, I spot something on the ceiling. Looks like a hatch. A way out.

I crawl over beneath it. The hinges must be on the other side. It's just a flat metal plate. I try shoving it open, but it doesn't budge. So I scramble onto my back and push up with my feet. Nothing.

It won't work. You can't get away.

I hold back from screaming my lungs out. I don't want to get Starks's attention.

It won't be long.

"Shut up!"

He won't keep you. You're not what he wants. He only likes boys.

There are no cracks around the edges of the hatch, no way to see what's up there.

"What is this place?"

He calls it the pit. It's where he breaks you.

I swallow back my panic. I can't fall apart now. Just keep talking.

"Like the way he broke you?"

Silence. Is this how Starks turned the smiling Leo on the MISSING poster into the creature he is now?

Think, Jane! Nobody's coming to save you. If only I still had my ring. They'll be searching for me, but won't have any idea where to look. I don't even know where I am. How long was I running blindly? How far? The middle of nowhere, Starks said.

No. I'm on my own.

I reach out to touch the light, but it doesn't give off any heat.

My shadow finally did it. Leo never could manage to kill me himself, so he delivered me to a pro to do it for him.

I shudder, leaning back against the wall.

Then I hear something. Holding my breath, I stare at the hatch. Is Starks up there? Coming back for me?

There it is again. A rustling sound. So close.

But not from above.

I catch movement over by that heap of blankets at the other end of this pit. There's something under there.

What? Mice? Rats? Or worse?

What am I locked in here with?

I scramble back as far as I can, pressed against the wall in this corner of the cell. Shaking and panting. Bracing myself. A scream rising in my throat.

Something comes out from beneath the blankets.

My heart seems to stop.

I see hair. Eyes. A face. It looks corpselike in the blue glow.

"Help me," it says.

43

The pit.

This is where he breaks you.

Billy Hughes knows that better than me.

"How long have you been here?" I asked, after he told me his name.

"Don't know. What month is it?"

"January. The thirtieth."

"Still January? Last day I remember was the tenth."

Nearly three weeks for Billy. But not always down here.

"What's up there?" I asked.

He went silent for so long then, I didn't think he was going to answer. The eerie blue light made him look frozen and half dead.

"Bad place," he mumbled finally. "Bad things."

It took a while getting it out of him. This cell is hidden under the floor of a small house. The trappers' hut.

I made him describe it to me, down to the smallest detail he could remember, so I could build a mental image of the layout. Where the door is, the boarded-up windows. There's a woodstove, a table, a long workbench with all kinds of tools.

I kept him talking for a while. It seemed to calm him a bit, and helped keep my own panic from swallowing me up.

Billy Hughes is from Mill Valley, farm country in the interior, a long way from Edgewood. He's thirteen. Same age Leo Gage was when he was taken.

"How did you end up here?" I asked. He stayed quiet on me a long moment. "You don't have to say if you don't want."

"I should've run," he whispered. "I would've, but the bird stopped me."

Billy was walking home from the grocery store on a back road in the valley when a truck drove past him. He was just a half mile from his family's farm. The truck went over a hill and out of sight. When Billy got to the top of the hill he saw that the truck had pulled over to the side. There was a tall bald man in a strange uniform standing beside it, looking up into the trees. "Lost my bird," he said. "He's big and black. You seen him?"

Billy just shook his head and kept on going. Then he spotted it, hopping out from the underbrush onto the road straight ahead. A crow, dragging one wing in the dirt.

"That him?" Billy called back to the man.

"Yeah, that's Blackjack," he said. "Looks like he's hurt. Don't let him get away." The bird kept hopping, toward the far side of the road, so Billy rushed to cut him off. The crow stopped right at Billy's feet, one wing hanging limp.

"Don't scare him off," the man told him. "Don't move. Does it look like his wing's broken?"

Billy was staring down at the bird when the man reached him.

"Then it was like I got hit by lightning," he said. "I saw a big flash. Felt like burning under my skin. And . . . I woke up here. But it wasn't lightning. He's got an electric gun."

"I know. It's a stun gun. That's how he got me too."

Lexi was right. Starks uses the crow as a lure. The Amazing Blackjack knows a lot of tricks.

"What's with this blue light?"

"He says it's a special kind of light—ultraviolet. It kills germs. He likes things clean."

That explains why it stinks of ammonia in here.

Billy quit talking after that. Now he's just crouched under the hatch. I won't press him to tell me what's happened to him since he got caught—really don't want to know. His own MISSING poster must be buried somewhere in Dad's task force files, with all the other lost kids and runaways.

I hug my knees to my chest, trying to conserve body heat.

If it was just me alone in here I'd be freaking out of my mind by now. I don't know, maybe it's being a cop's daughter, but I feel like I have to step up and take charge for both of us. So I tell him what must be my worst lie ever.

"Hey, Billy. We'll get out of this. Just hang in there."

"I'm never getting out," Billy mumbles. "Gonna die here."

Then he retreats to his end of the pit.

My turn to go silent. I'm trying to believe my own lie. There's got to be some kind of chance. Look at how many times I've cheated death. The odds were always against me. Like Lexi says, I'm the girl with nine lives. So maybe I've got one more life in me. Have to fight for it.

I run through all the self-defense moves Dad ever taught me. Eye gouges, throat chops, head butts, kicks, bites, punches, elbows and knees. Whatever it takes to survive, he said. I remember the moves, but that was all so easy back in the community center, practicing on a man-shaped dummy that didn't fight back. Starks is more than a foot taller than me, with a longer reach and a stun gun. I don't have anything to use as a weapon—no keys, pen or nail file. All I've got is me.

My breath shudders out, and I have to swallow back the sobbing rising in my chest. What did Dad tell me? *Don't let fear freeze you.* I'm trying, but it's so hard.

Do something! I yell at myself. Whatever it takes.

So I find a rough patch on the floor and start scraping my fingernails on it. I want them ragged. I need sharp claws for scratching.

Nails, teeth and knuckles. The only weapons I've got.

I can feel Leo nearby, watching. Waiting.

Huddled in my corner, I try to plan. Visualizing the room above me, I play out an attack in my head. No way I'd make it to the door with him still standing. Go for the workbench, the tools. Grab something. But any way I play it, I end up dead.

I can smell the fear in my cold sweat.

I test my new claws against my palms. Jagged and sharp.
Whatever it takes.

If Dad could see me now. I've really become the Bull-dog's daughter.

A distant thud breaks the silence. Billy whimpers. I hold my breath, listening. Leaning on the cement wall, I feel vibrations.

Footsteps!

What do I do? What do I do?

More steps. Coming closer.

He's there! Standing above me.

Metal clashes against metal, deafening inside the cramped space. Sounds like—unlocking!

I lie back down, just how I was when I came to. How he left me.

Shaking inside, I force myself to keep still.

Whatever happens, don't move.

Play dead!

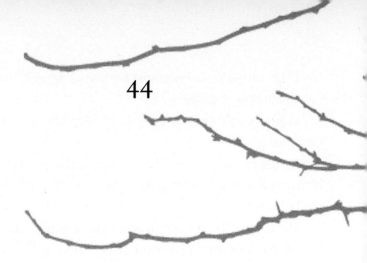

44

The hatch squeals open.

Through my closed eyelids I can see the brightening, smell fresh air.

"Get up!" Starks says.

I stay still. Breathing slow. Swallowing back a scream.

"Move!"

Shivering deep inside. Don't let it show.

Hands grab my ankles near the opening, dragging me out. I fight the instinct to kick and struggle, going limp as I'm pulled up and out of the pit. The back of my head hits the edge.

I don't flinch. Not showing it. Keeping my eyes shut.

He lets my legs fall to the floor.

"This can be quick and painless." Starks stands over me. "Or not. Up to you."

Sounds like Leo—*I tried to make it quick, painless.* This is where he learned that. I can feel him close by.

I want to scream. Run. But no—

Stay limp. Don't move. Not yet.

There's a loud screech somewhere to my left. Blackjack. The crow's over where the bench should be, if I've got my directions right.

Grab a tool. Anything.

"Get up!"

He kicks me in the ribs. I grunt, but keep still. Eyes shut.

Wait. Don't move.

"You got a little taste of what my stunner can do. It'll knock you out, or I can make it last longer. Till you wish you were dead."

A fist locks onto my right wrist, dragging me across the floor.

"You're gonna talk." His voice is ice cold. "Tell me what you know."

I struggle not to flinch. Not to pull away.

Wait! Not yet!

He lets go. I can feel him bending over me. His hands gripping under my arms, lifting me.

Not yet.

He's up close. His stale coffee breath in my face.

Now!

My eyes fly open. I swing my arms up and go for his face. Scratching wildly. Digging my claws in and raking down before he can block me.

Starks shoves me away. I stumble back and hit something hard with my tailbone.

The crow's shrieking. The room's spinning on me.

I whip my head around, trying to find— Behind me, the bench! I lunge for the nearest thing. A hammer. Grabbing it, I spin back.

He's coming! Blood trailing from his cheek and forehead. I raise the hammer to strike. Starks rushes me, his arm up to block. I swing, jumping to the side at the last second.

The hammer bangs off his skull as he crashes me into the bench. I fall to my knees, sliding away from under him. Still got the hammer. I stagger to my feet, turning to face him.

Too late!

He's on me, taking me down. The back of my head bounces off the floor. I try to move, but he pins me.

Feels like my skull's split apart. Can't see straight.

His bald head hangs above me. Those black eyes—black holes—lock onto mine.

He's dripping on me. The blood runs from deep cuts on his face and from where the hammer gouged a chunk of flesh from behind his ear.

My head rolls to the side, my vision spinning. I see black wings in the air. The crow's screeching. There's a table. A stove. A door on the far side of the hut. And a head sticking up from a hole in the floor.

Run, kid!

Starks presses his knee into my chest, holding me still as he rips something out of his pocket. I try to raise my head, but he snags my hair and yanks it down.

What's that he's got?

I catch the lightning flash a split second before he hits me with it.

The jolt tears through me. White-hot spikes. My whole body spasms, seizing up. Breathless.

Shaking wildly, I nearly throw him off me. For a moment the stun gun breaks contact. I suck in a gasp of air. My arms and legs jump and twitch.

Starks sits on my chest, trapping my shoulders down with his knees. He holds the gun in front of my eyes, finger on the trigger, the jagged electric charge sizzling.

I beg silently, Let me black out, go numb.

Let go, says Leo's voice in my head. *Give up.*

My ghost is so close. Almost touching me.

Let go.

Then Starks jams the gun under my jaw. My body convulses. Lightning flaring behind my eyes.

I let my last breath out in a ragged scream. Screaming inside: Stop! Stop! Help me!

Begging for an end.

Help me!

Then I feel him, my ghost. His touch. Crawling inside me now.

Starks keeps on shocking me. But it's so far away—my pain, my panic, my body.

Every part of me is shaking violently.

Everything but my shadow. I watch as it stretches out from my shuddering left hand. Flowing through the air, the five-fingered shadow reaches out for Starks.

The dark hand presses up against his chest. Starks glances down and tries to brush it off.

His confused look turns to shock as those shadow fingers dig in, passing through his jacket. Sinking deeper till the dark hand is buried wrist-deep in him.

Starks's face goes rigid and he tries to pull away. But it won't let go.

I can just barely feel that hand moving inside him, as if it's an extension of me. Like an extra limb I never knew I had.

Starks drops the stun gun, breaking the current. He grabs at the black wrist growing out of his chest that stretches from me to him.

The crow's shrieking now, swooping low. I feel the rush of its wings as it passes near.

Those shadow fingers are searching inside Starks. The hand cups around something that throbs in its grasp. His heart.

The ranger claws at his chest.

Leo's voice rises up in my head, a scream of pain and rage only I can hear.

My shadow's hand closes in a fist. Squeezing tight!

Starks goes stiff on top of me, back arching, neck straining. Dark eyes bulging. His face clenches in agony as he shrieks.

The noise is deafening inside me and out, with the crow screeching too, as if it's being torn apart.

Starks drops off me, hitting the floor with a thud as my shadow crushes his lifeless heart in its grasp.

Then, silence. Only my ragged breathing.

Random twitches and electric shivers run through me. But I can't make myself move. Not an inch. My head is rolled to one side. I'm staring straight at Starks. At those dead eyes.

Finally, that dark arm connecting us pulls out from his chest. It drifts away from me like smoke.

Something else comes into view. Billy stands stunned and wide-eyed, holding the crow in his hands. The bird is limp, its neck bent back at an impossible angle.

As I'm looking up at Billy, I see him turn red. But not just him. Everything's going red on me.

"You're bleeding," he says. "From your eyes."

I'm fading fast.

I see two kids watching me now. One dark, one light. Leo and Billy. Dead and alive.

The dead one has the last word.

Now you're mine.

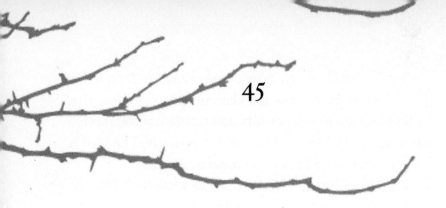

45

That's me on the floor. My body. I'm looking down at it, from the outside.

My legs are still twitching from the shock of the stun gun. But the lights have gone out behind my eyes.

I rise up, weightless. The ghost me.

From above I see the two corpses, mine and Starks's, side by side, facing each other. Empty shells now. The only living thing left here is Billy, shaking my shoulder.

Leaving my body behind, I pass through the roof of the hut. Into the night.

The rain falls through me. I can't feel the cold or the wind. Can't feel anything but the *pull* of the sky. Like it's calling out to me.

Then I'm flying, higher and higher, till I can see the whole town under me. The streetlights look like stars fallen to the ground, lined up in constellations linking everything together. I spot my house, a yellow glow at the end of a string of stars.

I feel a rush of sadness. At leaving Mom and Dad, Lexi and everything I've ever known.

But there's no going back. No goodbyes.

The lights below fade as Edgewood falls farther away. Looking up to see where I'm going, I find nothing. No stars. No sky.

Just infinite blackness. *The Divide.*

It pulls me away from the world with its own dark gravity, surrounding me, swallowing me.

I've never felt so hopeless and heartsick.

I know this time death is forever.

But I'm not alone.

A pair of eyes opens in the blackness, glimmering.

There's no getting away from Leo. But I'm not scared anymore. He's already taken everything from me. And here in the dark I have no shadow left to betray me.

Now I'm mad! For all the pain he caused. For my stolen life.

He glides closer. Looking the same as when he haunted me. Still starving thin, wearing his hooded sweatshirt.

The shine of his eyes casts him in a pale amber glow.

You came back to me.

He sounds so sad and small. Not a ghost's voice now, just a kid's.

"You made me." My words echo from my mind to his.

But you belong with me. You're mine.

"I never was! And never will be."

I'll fight him even if there's nothing left to fight for. Even if it's forever.

But I found you, when you were lost. I kept you safe. Kept you close.

"I wasn't yours to keep!" My shout booms like thunder through the Divide.

And it wakes something else up in this dead place.

A spark of light in the distance, behind Leo. It's so small I don't want to look away in case I lose it. As I'm watching, it grows from a spark to a star—the only one here.

The sight of that little ember ignites a feeling of hope. And I remember. I know that light. What it means.

Leo follows my gaze.

No! he cries. *I won't let you.*

"Don't you know what that is?"

It's a lie. It burns. Panic in his voice.

The oncoming light has grown in the dark.

My anger is fading, with the promise of that glowing brightness. I feel almost sorry for my ghost now, spending forever in this graveyard of souls.

"Come with me," I say.

The light widens into a blazing white eye.

I can't. It hurts.

"The light sets you free."

Not me. He's shaking his head, eyes wide with fear.

"You have to let go of all the bad stuff. The hut. The pit. Him. All your pain. Let go."

Can't. Never.

"Why not?"

He reaches out and grabs me. *Here's why—*

Even in these ghost bodies, he feels solid. But so cold. The contact pulls me into his mind.

This is where he keeps his worst memories locked away.

Images from his past flash by, burning into my mind's eye. Carrying with them the feel of these moments, every sound, touch and smell.

The hut. And the pit. But this time I see them through Leo's eyes.

I watch because I can't shut it out. I'm a prisoner to his past, just like he is.

After he is taken, he wakes up in a strange bed, cold and confused. In a dark room with smoke-stained walls. He's got no clothes on, and he hurts in places he's never been hurt before. Then he sees the bald ranger standing over him.

Later, locked in the pit. Left here until the monster returns.

Then starved till he begs for scraps. Beaten, and worse.

Till he gives up thinking of ever getting away. Because he can never go home again. Not after what's been done to him, what he's been forced to do. Never see his mother or let her see this disgusting *thing* he's become. She could never love him now.

He's kept in the pit so long he forgets who he is. Till he's nothing but a shadow.

He's glad when death comes. So he can fly away, leaving his broken body and this nightmare world. Flying so far he leaves even the stars behind.

He likes it here in this void, where nobody can see him and he can't see himself. He hides in the dark and feels nothing for the longest time.

But he's still tied to the place where he's buried, his hidden grave. That's how he spots the little soul, escaping from the town where his bones lie. It's like a firefly in the blackness. He holds it and keeps it close.

The rush of images cuts off.

I find myself back in the Divide. Staring into his eyes.

You came, he says. *And made me feel something that didn't hurt. I can't lose you!*

While I was trapped in his memories, the light has become a perfect round moon, so close now I could dive right into it. I can make out my own ghost body in its shine. My pale skin reflecting the glow.

I'm shocked to see how the light dies on Leo. He stays a shadow, lit only by the flares of his eyes.

You see now? he says. *What I am? Why I can't go?*

The pain of his memories is still raw in me. Like I lived it with him. Died with him. I have no words.

Stay with me. Please, he begs.

I feel the light calling to me with its perfect sunshine. So beautiful. Its warmth melts away all my anger and grief for my stolen life.

Leo moves closer, as if he can stop me now. All he's ever given me is pain and fear. But I can't hate this sad and broken soul.

"Let me show you," I say. "If you can just let go, it will only hurt for a second. I promise."

You're lying. It burns forever. I won't let you go. Don't make me hurt you.

"You can't hurt me now."

Because caught in the shine I have no shadow left. And he has no power over me.

It's time to go.

As I stretch my hand toward the light, it reaches out for me. Curling around my fingers with a glowing fog, slipping down my wrist and arm with a thrill of pure white heat.

Leo grabs my other hand.

He's locked on tight. Still, I'm stronger than the first time he stole me from the light. And now that I've seen my shadow's real face, I'm not afraid.

I know what I have to do. For both of us.

He won't let go, so I won't let him go either. I grasp his hand tight.

This is the only way to make him see.

I open myself up to the brightness, letting it fill me, and its current flows through me to Leo.

When it passes from my hand to his I feel his shock. He struggles to break free.

NO! His shout echoes across the Divide.

The light burns into that blackest place where his memories are locked away, and my ghost body ignites as I feed the fire into him.

Leo screams in wild terror as every horror is dragged out of him in flames.

And even with his soul on fire he fights to keep hold of these nightmare things. Like he's nothing without his darkness.

But finally his screams quiet to sobs as he gives up and lets himself burn through.

When the blazing brightness softens again I can see him clearly. With the darkness stripped away from him, he looks smaller, younger. His eyes are warm, the color of honey.

I let go of his hand as the light takes Leo, swirling around him.

Sorry, he says in a sleepy whisper. *Sorry, Jane.*

As he drifts toward the whiteness of that perfect moon, I move to follow.

But something in me holds back. Why? The glow is the sweetest, most beautiful thing I've ever known. But it's not calling to me like before.

Something else is.

I start drifting, away from the light, caught in a tide. I watch it shrink to an eye, an ember, a spark.

And then I'm falling. Slowly at first. Out of the empty night of the Divide and into a sky filled with stars.

I dive through the clouds and past them into the rain below. I see a familiar constellation of lights down there.

Edgewood grows large beneath me, the ground rushing up.

But I'm not afraid. I know where I'm going.

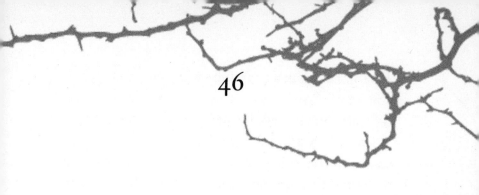

46

I slept for six days straight after the surgery, in a medically induced coma to help me heal. A sleep too deep for dreams, or nightmares.

First thing I saw when I opened my eyes was Lexi, slouched in a chair beside my hospital bed, flipping through a movie magazine.

She jumped up.

"Jane? You're awake? Can you hear me?"

I could. But my words took a long time coming. My throat was dry as a desert, and I had to focus to get my mouth working again.

I looked up into her beautiful dark eyes. Never thought I'd see them again.

"Can you speak?" Lexi stood over me, so worried and anxious. "Say something!"

I could see her wondering—Is she a vegetable now? Is there brain damage?

"Jane, do you know who I am?"

My lips parted, but I couldn't make a sound.

"Do you know me?" she asked.

Finally, I managed a scratchy whisper.

"Sis . . . ter."

"What?" She bent down, her ear close to my lips.

"Creep . . . Sis . . . ter."

Lexi leaned back, smiling. She was so choked up it took a minute before she could make her own voice work again.

"Don't go anywhere. Let me run and get your mom. She just went for coffee downstairs."

But before she left I had to make sure about something.

"Hey," I whispered in my sandpaper voice. "I'm . . . not dead . . . right?"

"Not dead."

I lay there stunned by every breath I took, every heartbeat. Everything that said: not dead.

A lot happened while I slept those six days.

Billy Hughes was returned to his family in Mill Valley. He'd been missing three weeks. What he went through during that time I don't have to imagine. I saw enough when I shared my ghost's memories.

When the investigators dug into Starks's past they found no criminal history, until they uncovered his juvenile record, which had been sealed by law when he hit eighteen. Growing up, he'd been arrested for everything from indecent exposure to unlawful imprisonment, with some molestation charges that were dropped. By the time he became an adult he knew how to cover his tracks better, how not to get caught.

After a search of the hut and the surrounding woods they turned up no sign of other victims.

Then they found the map. Part of a park ranger's job is tracking wildlife. In Starks's computer they pulled up maps of animal migration patterns, nesting sites, dens and burrows. Another ranger who was called in to consult discovered something strange. There was a map showing the burrows of Western black-eared gophers. An animal that's been extinct for over a century. And the location for one burrow matched the burial site of Leo Gage. When they checked out the other "gopher" sites they found more bodies.

Five more lost boys. The graves were spread out deep in the forests of Raincoast National Park. The police think Starks kept track of the sites so he could visit his victims and relive what he'd done to them.

His trappers' hut is located just outside Edgewood but hidden in dense woods. I ran a crazy unconscious marathon that night to get there.

They did an autopsy to determine the ranger's cause of death. Dad said I didn't need to hear about that, but I wouldn't let it go.

Starks's death was declared a cardiac arrest, with a contributing heart defect. When they cut him open they discovered that the walls of his heart had totally collapsed. There was no external trauma to the chest, so the coroner couldn't explain why the heart appeared to have been crushed flat. He'd never seen anything like it.

When it came time for me to explain what happened that night—how I ended up in the hut in the woods—

I kept my lies real simple. I told them the last thing I remembered was passing out in our bathroom at home. Then I must have gone sleepwalking, gotten out of the house. For everything past that, I claimed I had a killer case of amnesia, no memory of what, how or why everything went down the way it did. I had my recent surgery to blame for that.

I left it to Dad and the task force cops to come up with some theories.

Their best guess was this: Starks must have been out driving and spotted me sleepwalking down the middle of the street. I would have been easy prey in my unconscious state. But what they couldn't explain, what didn't make sense to them, was why he'd abduct a girl. Because predators like Starks almost always stick to a very specific type of victim. He was into boys. This left the profilers puzzled. But as far as the task force was concerned, whatever Starks's motives were in grabbing me, he took them to the grave.

Billy Hughes came to visit me in the hospital a few days after I woke. His mother was with him, but he asked to see me alone.

He was all cleaned up now, hiding behind the mousy brown hair that hung down over his eyes, still looking thin and sickly from his captivity.

He stood by the foot of my bed, head bowed. When he spoke it was just a mumble, as if he was scared of waking something up that would be better left lying.

"I thought you were dead," he said. "Back there, that night."

I *was* dead, but I didn't tell him that. "I thought so too."

He crossed his arms, rubbing them like he was cold.

"You saved me," he muttered, staring at the floor, at the walls, everywhere but at me.

"Yeah, well, you saved me right back. So we're even."

Dad told me how it was Billy who called for help using Starks's cell phone. Billy couldn't tell them where we were exactly because he didn't know. So they located us with the GPS on the phone.

The paramedics got my heart beating again in the ambulance. Fighting with Starks and getting my skull bounced off the floor made the nail in my head shift enough to cause the brain bleed that flatlined me in the hut.

Billy leaned in a little closer now and spoke in a hushed voice. "I didn't tell them."

"About what?" I asked.

"How you killed him."

Our eyes met, and it was like a whole conversation happened without us having to say a word. He'd seen what my shadow did to Starks.

I nodded. "And you dealt with that rotten bird."

"Wasn't hard," he said. "I grew up on a farm. A crow's neck snaps the same as a chicken's."

I tried to see in Billy's eyes if the damage was too deep. Was he going to change the way Leo had? The victim becoming the monster? I knew it would be a long way back from the hell Billy had gone through. But he wouldn't be alone, hiding in the dark like Leo. Billy had a chance.

"Anyway," he said. "I came here because . . . I just needed to make sure you were real, that I didn't imagine you. Doesn't make any sense, I guess."

"Yeah, it does. I know."

I know. Because when our universe shrank to the size of a cage, all we had was each other. It felt like I was in that pit for days, but I found out later it was only one endless night.

Billy stepped back from my bed then, like he was ready to go. But he had one last question.

"It sounds crazy. But sometimes I get scared, thinking I'm really still down there. You know, that I never got out, and I'm just dreaming all this." He was shaking his head and hugging his arms tighter. "So I need to know—is it really over?"

He was asking for himself, for his own nightmare, but I answered him for mine too.

"It's over."

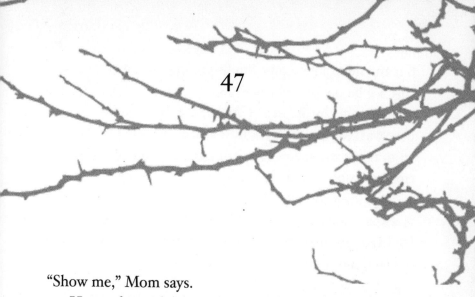

47

"Show me," Mom says.

Home from the hospital, I'm sitting at the kitchen table eating breakfast after my first night's sleep in my own bed for over a month. They took out the stitches yesterday.

"It's not pretty," I warn her.

She's been washing dishes, and dries her hands off on a towel as she comes over.

Dad's sitting across from me, blinking sleepily over his coffee. He's out of uniform on his day off, wearing a ragged old wrestling-team T-shirt.

I take off the wool cap I'm wearing to cover up the scars on my head. Mom leans in close.

"Seems to be healing up nicely," she says. "How does it feel?"

"Stings a little if I frown or raise my eyebrows. Besides that, it just itches a lot."

Of course, it goes deeper. My manual dexterity is still recovering. My handwriting's a mess, my typing is terrible. Buttoning and zipping things is still kind of tricky, but the neurologist says I'm improving on schedule. He's sure I'll be back to normal soon.

No other problems. I mean, I'm no dumber than I ever was. My senses are still sharp. I can smell the lemon from the dishwashing liquid and feel Mom's warm fingertips on my bare scalp. I don't think I've lost any memories.

But something's gone, and it's hard to describe what's missing. It's like the sound of the rain, that never-ending background of white noise that you forget to hear after a while, the way you tune out the sound of your own breathing. And you don't really notice it till it stops. So what I feel is like the absence of a feeling that's always been there. Because my ghost is gone, and that takes some getting used to.

Now I've just got Mom watching over me.

"You know," she says, resting her hands on my shoulders, "when you were really little, my bald little baby, I couldn't get enough of your smell. I was always sniffing your smooth head. It was like fresh cream with a hint of vanilla."

I bend my neck back to look up at her.

"Thanks, Mom."

"For what?"

I shrug. "For saving me, more times than you even know."

She leans down to kiss my head.

Across the table the constable has got us under surveillance. I brush my fingers over my mangled scalp.

"What do you think, Dad? Could I win the Bride of

Frankenstein beauty pageant? Or will I be zombie prom queen this year?"

"Be proud of your scars, Boo. They tell your story—what fights you won and lost. And when your hair grows in, who's gonna know but us? Just be glad you don't have to look at this busted mess in the mirror every morning."

He taps the fallen bridge of his nose and gives me his best snarling-dog grin, zigzag eyebrow raised high.

Dad always says thank God I got my looks from Mom and didn't take after him. But with my scars it's like we go together, a matching pair. Maybe I should be proud of the story they tell, what they say about me.

That I'm the Bulldog's daughter.

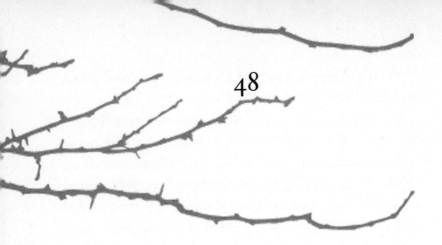

48

"Is that me?" I ask.

The girl in the mirror stares back, looking shocked.

"The new you," Lexi says.

Two months after they shaved my head for the surgery, all I've got is an inch of peach fuzz. And now it's dyed midnight black.

"How does it look on top?" I ask. "Can you see anything?"

I'm sick of wearing hats, but when my fuzz was blond you could see my scary scars.

Lexi gives her dye job an inspection from every angle.

"Nothing. It's perfect camouflage."

I run my fingers through it, feeling the hidden lines and bumps on my scalp.

We're up in her room above the garage, where she's worked her magic on my hair. Black Magic, that's what this shade is called.

"Now we really do look like sisters," I say, seeing our reflection and our raven-black hair.

I'm not her only makeover project. Lexi's room has been transformed, and the "wall of death" is gone.

Lexi's the only one who knows the whole truth about what went on in the hut, and afterward in the Divide. She's my secret vault.

The rest of her walls are bare too; the photo gallery of her old life in sunny San Diego has been stripped away. She's still editing her own home movies from back then, splicing the footage together a thousand different ways, trying to figure it all out, why her father left and everything fell apart. But she's given up on finding a final version. Now she says, "No matter how I cut it I can't change the ending."

"So what's the new decor going to be?" I glance around. It looks like somebody's moving out, or moving in.

"Don't know yet. I'm starting from scratch."

Lexi's been riding a high lately. Her minimovie *A Thousand Words for Rain* is getting some good buzz online. In the end, she went without the music by Max. Instead, she used the nature sounds we recorded and let the rain speak for itself.

She's deleted Max. Every photo, music file, message and video. Erased all trace of him. But as with any addiction, she has to kick it one day at a time.

Lexi holds up a little hand mirror so I can check out the back of my head. Not bad.

"Now let me finish," she says. "I'm thinking blush, some gloss, a little eyeliner. Then you're good to go."

Where I'm going is over to Shipwrecks. To meet

Ryan. It's not a date, just coffee. But tell that to my shaky nerves.

I sit back and let Lexi do her magic on me.

Can I handle this? Is it too soon after all that's happened? I don't know.

But I am so ready!

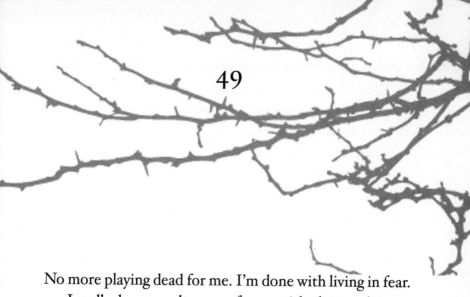

49

No more playing dead for me. I'm done with living in fear.

I walk down to the waterfront, with the sun hot on my back and the sky a clear, true blue all the way to the horizon. The rainy season is over, and it feels like the whole town is waking from the longest dream.

Fishing boats are heading out, swarmed by seagulls. The water is a calm green-blue. The same shade as Ryan's eyes.

I catch my reflection in a store window and barely recognize myself. Who are you now? I ask the girl in the glass. Lexi's not the only one starting from scratch. I'm still getting used to being alone inside my own head.

I look at my shadow stretched out in front of me on the sidewalk. It doesn't look back. Nothing hiding there.

Up ahead, Shipwrecks comes into view.

I spot Ryan sitting at the window. There's a small potted plant beside him on the counter, the love log. I can tell what the plant is by the shape of its pointy leaves: aloe vera. The kind they call the crocodile's tongue.

I smile. He came, and he brought me tongue.

I take a moment to just breathe.

Closing my eyes, I turn to catch the bright sunshine on my face and remember the promise of that other light. Waiting for me. Someday.

I open my eyes.

But not today.

Graham McNamee won the Edgar Award for *Acceleration*. He's also the author of the thriller *Bonechiller*. Both were named ALA Best Books for Young Adults. Graham McNamee lives on Canada's Rain Coast. He says, "*Beyond* was inspired by my mother, who died when she was a little girl and was brought back to life."